The Mound Street Tigers

The Mound Street Tigers

Ernest Stadvec

To order additional copies of this book, contact:
Essco Publishing
378 S. Van Buren Ave.
Barberton, OH 44203
1-877-318-1555

Chapter 1

Four young boys rode their bicycles onto a narrow dirt road leading through a dense woods toward a small lake. Steve, a small boy wearing thick glasses, stopped at a sign in the middle of the narrow path. He pointed at it.

"Hey, you guys, look at this."

Two of the boys following, Arnold, tall and skinny, Emil short, stocky, swerved to keep from hitting Steve. A fourth boy, Boris, chubby with a shock of black hair, skidded into the bushes to avoid the others.

Arnold and Emil wheeled their bikes closer to the sign.

"No trespassing," Arnold read.

"Armed guards patrolling," Emil added as he pointed to each word.

Boris climbed out of the bushes. "You guys trying to kill me or something?"

Arnold had a worried look on his face. "No, but whoever put up this sign might."

Boris brushed the leaves off his clothes. "What sign?"

Emil pointed to the No Trespassing sign. "That sign."

"Armed guards patrolling," Steve said.

"It wasn't up the other day we were here," Arnold said.

"I know who put it up," Emil said. "I heard my Dad telling one of his buddies a guy from Cleveland rented the old Miller farm and this pond is on the Miller property."

Arnold was already on his bike.

"I'm getting outta here. I ain't getting my butt shot off just to go swimming."

Emil was right behind Arnold.

"Me neither."

Boris took a close look at the sign.

He went to the edge of the water, scooped up two handfuls of mud and plastered them over the sign.

"We been swimming here a long time. Nobody's scaring Boris the Great away."

The three boys watched as Boris stripped down to his baggy underwear. He kicked off his tenner shoes, then ran toward the water yelling, "Last one in's a monkey's uncle."

"Why not?" Emil said. He took off his clothes and followed Boris into the water.

Steve took of his clothes. He folded them in a neat pile and then took of his glasses and laid them on top of his clothes. He jumped in after Emil and Boris.

Arnold hesitated. He kept glancing at the sign with the mud covered letters.

"I don't know about this. I don't want to get shot."

"Aw c'mon in," Emil yelled. "Nobody's gonna shoot some kids just having fun."

Arnold took off his clothes. He waded into the water while watching the woods.

"Jeez it's cold," he said folding his arms across his chest clutching each shoulder.

Emil splashed him. "Aw stop complaining."

Arnold waded toward the shorter boy. "I'm getting you for that."

Boris climbed out of the water. He took hold of a rope tied to a tree limb and backed up as far as he could. He ran forward letting out a wild Tarzan yell as he leaped into the air at the edge of the bank swinging out over the water.

"Look out below you slime balls. The king of swing is coming to get you."

Just as he reached the end of his swing, two shots cut through the dense woods. Boris let go of the rope. He grabbed his chest with both hands.

"They got me."

He fell, arms and legs flailing. He never came up. The others stared at where Boris went into the water.

Steve swam toward the bubbles.

"Somebody shot Boris."

"I knew it. I knew it," Arnold said. "We should'a gone home." He swam over and dove under after Emil.

The three boys popped up out of the water, sputtering and breathing hard.

"I can't find him," Steve said gasping for air.

"Me neither," Emil said between taking deep breaths.

"I knew it. I knew it," Arnold said coughing out water.

"Shut up. Keep looking," Emil said then went under again. Steve and Arnold followed.

After several long moments, the three boys surfaced one after the other.

"I can't find him," Steve was able to say between gasps for air.

"We gotta find him." Emile managed to say then dove under again.

Arnold was breathing hard. "I knew it. We shoulda gone home."

"Keep looking," Steve said then dove under again. Arnold followed.

The three boys surfaced one after the other.

Steve shook his head. He wiped tears from his eyes.

"Our good buddies gone."

"This is awful," Arnold said. "We shoulda gone home. Now we lost our friend."

Steve swam to the shore. "We got to get some help."

Arnold kept shaking his head. "What we telling his Ma and Pa?"

"Tell em I'll be home for supper."

The three boys turned to see Boris grinning at them.

"Don't stop now. I liked what you guys were saying. Tell me more."

The three boys stared at him.

"It's a ghost," Arnold croaked.

"A fat ghost," Emil said backing away.

Boris laughed. "It's really me. I ain't no ghost and I ain't fat, maybe a little chubby."

"We thought you was fish food," Arnold said.

Boris laughed. "I sure had you dummies fooled. Boris the Great strikes again."

The three boys looked at each other.

"Get him." Steve yelled.

They gabbed Boris and ducked him under. He came up coughing and spitting out water. "You guys cut it out or I'm telling my Ma."

Two more shotgun blasts echoed through the woods. The three boys let go of Boris and listened.

"They're coming this way," Steve said.

Arnold waded toward the shore. "I knew it. They're coming to kill us."

"They'll murderize us," Boris wailed as he headed for the bank of the pond.

"Shut up you guys," Steve said. "Listen."

Two men were yelling as they got closer to the pond.

"You get him?"

"Naw, he ran toward the pond."

"Let's get over there. Maybe we can corner it."

"They're getting closer," Steve said heading for the shore. "Come on you guys. Let's go before they catch us here."

Arnold and Emil were right behind Steve as they scrambled up the bank, pulled on their clothes, then wheeled their bicycles into the thick underbrush where they hid.

The sound of the two men coming through the bushes was much closer to the pond. Arnold parted the bushes. He pointed to where Boris was trying to climb the muddy bank but kept slipping back into the water.

"Boris," Steve called out in a loud whisper. "They're getting closer. Stay in the water. Hide behind the bushes. We'll get your clothes and bike."

"I'll get his bike, you get his clothes," Arnold whispered to Emil. The two boys darted out of their hiding place. Arnold wheeled Boris's bike into the bushes.

"Hurry up Emil," Steve said keeping his voice low.

Emil scooped up Boris's clothes. He ran toward the bushes where the other boys were hiding. He dropped Boris's pants. He started back to get them.

"Leave em," Steve whispered. "We'll get them when they leave."

Emil made it back in to their hiding place just as the two men broke out of the bushes. One man was big with a pot belly while the second was a foot shorter with his belly hanging over his belt. Both carried shotguns. The big man wore baggy bib overalls spotted with grease, a blue denim shirt soaked with sweat, clodhopper high top shoes and a hat that once had been brown with sweat stains above the brim. The shorter one had on green work pants, a dirty white undershirt with stains of a couple of breakfasts on it, high top work shoes and a worn straw hat. Sweat ran off his round red face. He pulled a dirty red bandana from a hip pocket, took off his battered straw hat, wiped his face, then the top of his head and behind his neck.

"This chasing a chicken stealing fox through these hot woods ain't my idea of Summer fun," the shorter man said.

The big man wiped his sweating face with the sleeve of his shirt. "Mine neither. We wouldn't be out here you hadn't told Jimmy a red fox been stealing his chickens that's why we was twenty short when he wanted a count."

"I had to say something," the short fat man said. "We got a good thing going taking Jimmy's chickens selling them at Nick's place. Blaming the missing chickens on the red fox was the perfect cover for us."

The big man took off his battered hat. He wiped his face, neck and shaved head with a big rag he pulled out of his pocket.

"Yeah, but now we gotta shoot a red fox so Jimmy don't find out we been stealing his chickens." He put on his hat. "Jimmy wants to see some action. He wants us to whack that chicken stealing red fox real soon."

"It's gotta be a red one too cause you told him it was red fox," the short fat man said.

"We saw one. You had a good shot. You missed," the big man said.

"It was a brown one anyway. We need a red fox."

"I don't care we see a green fox, a yellow fox, or even a purple one," the big man said. "We shoot any fox we can, paint it red, show it to Jimmy. He's from Cleveland. He won't know the difference."

The short man shook his head. "Whoever heard of shooting a fox then painting it red to look like red fox."

"There's always a first time."

The short man shook his head again. "Sounds like a lot of trouble to me. We know there's red fox in these woods. All we gotta do is track it down, shoot it, we're home free, off the hook with Jimmy."

"I ain't chasin nothing down in this heat," the big man said. "I'm done huntin for the day. Let's go back to the farm."

Chapter 2

Steve closed the branches. He turned to Emil and Arnold.

"You hear that? Those guys will shoot any fox they see."

"Then they'll paint him red," Arnold said in a hushed voice.

"Who are they?" Steve asked.

Arnold parted some branches, took a quick look then pulled back into the bushes.

"I know who they are," he said. "They work for Jimmy Roman, the guy everybody calls Jimmy the Cheese."

"Yeah," Emil whispered. "My Dad says that Roman guy rented the poolroom on Grand Street under the South Side Tavern. He's from here. Lives with his Mother. He came back to town about a month ago with those two guys out there. The big guy is Bosco Presnocki. The short fat one they call Usual."

"I heard they all just got out of reform school," Arnold whispered.

Emil looked out again.

"My Dad says Jimmy Roman is connected to a Cleveland gang where his Uncle is a big shot."

Steve took another look through the bushes at the two men who sat on the bank of the pond under a shade tree with their backs resting against the trunk.

"What they doing way out here in the country?" Steve asked in a low whisper.

Emil looked out again. "They took over the old Miller farm, nobody knows what they're doing out there.

"Probably something crooked," Arnold whispered.

"Hey," one of the men yelled.

"They found Boris," Emil said as all three of them looked through the bushes to where the two men had been sitting. Both men were standing looking down at something on the ground. Bosco picked up Boris's pants on the end of his shotgun barrel.

"They didn't get Boris," Steve whispered. "They got his pants."

Bosco waved the pants on the end of his shotgun barrel over his head. "Hey Usual, lookee here what I got."

Usual looked then laughed. "You ain't too good at shooting foxes but you sure bagged a big pair of pants.

"What you doing with em?"

"I'm takin em back to the farm for target practice."

Usual laughed again. "You can't hit a fox but you sure couldn't miss that big butt on those pants."

Just then, a red fox poked its head out of the bushes at the far edge of the pond.

Usual saw it. "Hey," he yelled pointing at it. "A red fox."

Bosco looked around. "Where, where?"

Usual lunged to where he left his shotgun. The red fox darted out of the bushes. It ran to Boris's lunch bag, grabbed it in its jaws then scurried back toward the bushes before Usual could get to his weapon. Bosco was still looking around when the fox ran right past him. It disappeared into the heavy underbrush while Bosco tried to get the big pair of pants off the barrel of his shotgun. Usual bent over, grabbed for his shotgun, lost his balance and fell flat on his stomach.

Steve turned to Emil and Arnold. "I don't think we have to worry about those two guys ever shooting the red fox."

Usual got up. He pointed at Bosco. "You dummy. It was the red fox. You coulda got him." Bosco grabbed Usual by the shirt front. He yanked him up until he was on his tiptoes.

"Who you calling a dummy you sawed off little tomato head. You saw it first. Why didn't you shoot it." Bosco let go of Usual's shirt. He pushed him back. "Just don't call me no dummy no more. Next time, I'll break your legs, and stuff em down your throat."

Usual backed up a few steps while rubbing his throat. "Aw come on Bosco. You know I'm a great kidder. I don't mean nothing when I'm kidding around like I just was."

Bosco grunted. He started walking toward the faint path leading into the woods. "I'm heading back to the farm. I'm done hunting for today."

Usual mopped his bald head, face and neck again, put on his straw hat and hurried into the woods after the big man. Once the two men disappeared into the woods, they started arguing again. Emil stood. He started to leave their hiding place. Steve held them back. "Let's wait till we can't hear them any more."

The boys waited until the arguing voices of the two men became fainter then disappeared. The three boys came out of their hiding place. They went over to the edge of the pond where Boris huddled in the water. His teeth were chattering as he hung onto an overhanging branch. Steve knelt on the bank. He leaned toward Boris. "It's Ok Boris. You can come out now. They're gone."

Boris had a scared look on his face. "You sure?"

Emil held out his hand. "Yeah, we're sure."

Arnold and Emil grabbed Boris's hands. They gave a heave. Boris pushed with his feet on the bank under the water. He propelled out of the water with him pushing and Emil and Arnold pulling. The two boys fell over backwards. Boris shot over their heads. He landed on the other side of them on his stomach. The three boys went over to him.

"You Ok?" Steve asked.

"Yeah, when I can breathe again," Boris managed to wheeze.

"Let's go home," Steve said.

Boris got up. He went over to the other boys. He looked around. "Where's my pants. Hey you guys come on, quit kiddin. Where's my pants?"

Emil looked around. "Where's Boris pants." He pointed to where he'd dropped them. "They were right there."

Boris had a look of panic on his face. "Where's my pants. I gotta find em. I can't go home without any pants on. What happened to my pants?"

The three boys exchanged glances. "I'm afraid they're gone Boris," Steve said. "Bosco, the big guy picked them up with his shot gun barrel. He told the other guy he was using your pants for target practice."

"He took your pants with him," Arnold said.

Boris was close to crying. "I can't go home in my underwear."

Steve thought for a moment. "You can wait here. We'll go home and get you another pair."

Boris shook his head. "My Ma will kill me if I lost my pants."

Arnold shrugged. "That's all we can do Boris."

"That's not all I can do," Boris said.

"Those guys aren't using my pants for target practice. I'm getting them back."

He looked around at the woods surrounding the pond. "Which way did they go?"

Steve pointed to the animal path the two men took.

"They're heading back to the old Miller farm. I heard them say," Arnold said.

"I'm going after them," Boris said. "I'm getting my pants back."

He ran to the animal path and disappeared in the dense underbrush.

"We got to catch Boris before he gets to the farm," Steve said. "Those guys will shoot him."

Steve started toward the path Boris had taken then turned toward Emil and Arnold. He motioned for them to follow. "You guys coming with me or not to save our buddy?"

Arnold hesitated, "I'm too young to die."

Emil grabbed his arm. "So am I. Let's go. We got to stop Boris before he gets to that farm."

The three boys hurried along the animal path making as little noise as possible. Steve stopped. He held up a hand motioning for Arnold and Emil to wait. He put a hand to one ear cupping it so he could hear better.

"What?" Arnold asked.

"Why we stopping?" Emil whispered.

Steve put a finger to his lips. "Shhh."

"Boris stopped," he whispered. I don't hear him anymore."

"He must have found those guys," Steve said.

"Or they found him," Arnold said.

Steve moved forward. He motioned Emil and Arnold to follow. "Let's go. Don't make any noise."

Emil and Arnold followed Steve through the almost grown overpath. Boris crouched behind a row of thick bushes at the edge of the barnyard. The three boys joined him.

"Where are those two guys who got your pants?" Steve asked keeping his voice low.

Boris pointed at the farm house. "They're in the kitchen drinking that stuff they're making in the barn."

Emil peered through the bushes. "They got a still in there. That must be where they make the bootleg whiskey Jimmy the Cheese and his gang make your Mom and Dad buy."

Boris got up. "They nailed my pants to the barn door. I'm getting them before they're shot to pieces."

Steve grabbed his arm. He pulled him down. "You can't just run out into the open. Those guys will shoot you."

Boris held his hands out to the others in what can I do gesture. "I got to get my pants back. I can't go home in my underwear."

"It's too risky," Steve whispered.

"How else can I get them," Boris said his voice breaking.

"We'll get your pants," Steve whispered, "I got a plan."

"What kind of plan?" Boris asked.

Steve pointed to the four old patched up chicken coops at the far edge of the barnyard set back a good ways from the farmhouse.

"We'll let the chickens out. We'll shoo them into the barnyard. They'll make enough racket those two guys will come out to see what's going on. While they are trying to get the chickens back into the hen houses, you run out, grab your pants off the barn doors. We'll catch up to you at the pond or out on the road."

Steve pointed to the chicken coops. "Arnold, you take the first one. You're the slowest runner so you can get into the bushes quicker. I'll take the next one. Emil, you open the last two. You're the fastest. When I give the signal like this," he made a chopping motion with his hand, "you guys open the doors, run the chickens out into the yard. When they're all out making a racket, Boris you run out grab your pants. We'll meet you at the pond or out on the road."

Steve turned to the three boys. "You guys ready." They all nodded. "Ok, let's do it."

Emil and Arnold followed Steve through the bushes bordering the barnyard until they were behind the chicken coops. Steve crept out of the bushes to the second coop. He gave the chopping motion with his hand. Each boy rushed over, opened the doors, went inside the hen houses and shooed the protesting chickens out into the barnyard. Within a few minutes, the barnyard was full of hopping, squawking, panicked chickens running around every which way. Emil, Arnold and Steve ran back into the bushes where Boris was waiting.

Steve gave Boris a push. "Go."

Bosco and Usual heard the commotion out in the barnyard. Bosco staggered to the open door. "The chickens are out," he yelled. "Somebody's trying to steal em." He grabbed his shotgun. "Let's go."

Usual snatched up his shotgun. He ran out the door after Bosco into the mass of terrified chickens. Bosco stopped. Usual ran into him. Both men fell into the middle of the clucking, hopping wing flapping chickens.

Boris ran right into the mass of chickens that were hopping all over Bosco and Usual as they tried to untangle themselves as they beat at the panicked birds. He went right past the two struggling men. Bosco grabbed his shot gun. "There he goes, get him. He's trying to steal the chickens."

Usual beat off the chickens hopping onto him, flapping their wings and squaking in his face. Both men struggled to their feet. Usual pointed to Boris who was dodging bunches of chickens running around in circles like he was avoiding tacklers as he ran towards the barn.

"He's heading toward the barn," Bosco yelled.

Both men ran after Boris who grabbed pants off the barn door. He looked around. He saw the two men kicking and yelling as they waded through out of control confused chickens. They were gaining on him. He ran into the barn past the gurgling hissing still.

Bosco raised his shotgun. "We got him now. There's no way out. Let him have it." He fired both barrels into the open barn. Usual stopped. He fired both barrels. "We got him," he yelled.

Both men ran into the barn. Bosco stopped at the still. Usual bumped into him. "What're you stopping for? He'll get away."

Bosco pointed at the big dial on top of the whiskey still's boiler. The pointer was steadily moving up into a red area marked Danger-Shut Boiler Down.

Usual stared at the pointer creeping into the red zone on the gauge. He turned and ran toward the open door. "You hit the safety valve," he yelled. "It's gonna blow."

Bosco's jaw dropped open. He started to say something but nothing came out. Then he was able to yell. "It's gonna blow," and was running right behind Usual.

Both men got to the door when the boiler gave out with a big burp and gurgle and an ominous hiss then blew apart. They were blown out into the barnyard right in the midst of the panicked mass of chickens.

Emil, Arnold and Steve felt the wave of the blast and ducked to the ground. They looked at each other and said at the same time, "Boris."

"He didn't make it," Arnold said with a catch in his voice.

Emil nodded. "He ran in the barn but never came out."

"Maybe he ran out the back end," Steve said.

Arnold shook his head. "Didn't you guys hear Bosco yell they got him. There was no other way out of the barn."

"I'm sure he got out before the place blew up," Steve said. "He's probably at the pond waiting for us. We better get out of here. The cops and firemen will come pretty soon. They find us here Bosco and Usual will blame everything on us."

The three boys started back toward the pond. Arnold stopped. "Maybe we should go look for Boris."

"Yeah, he might be hurt," Emil said.

Steve shook his head. "There were windows in that barn. I'm sure he got out. He's probably out on the road on his way home. Come on you guys, let's get out of here."

The three boys hurried back to the pond where they hid their bicycles. They rode over the narrow path through the woods as fast as they could. Just before they reached the paved road, they heard a familiar voice behind them. "Hey you guys, wait for me."

The three boys stopped. "It's Boris," Steve said. "He made it out."

Boris came out of the underbrush along the narrow path steering with one hand while holding something in his other. He pulled up beside the other boys. Before they could say anything he said, "I went out an open window in back of the barn."

Emil shook his head. "We thought you were done for when the barn blew up."

Boris thumped a fist on his chest. "Nobody can kill Boris the Great."

Steve pointed to Boris's other hand. "What you holding?"

Boris held up a stiff dried out dead cat by the tail. "Meet Arthur, my new pet cat."

Arnold moved in for a closer look. "A dead cat. You got a dead cat for a pet?"

Emil took a long look at the stiff dried out dead cat Boris held.

"That blast must of rattled his brain," he said.

Arnold backed away from Boris and the dead cat. "He's gone bananas," he said.

Boris stroked the dead cat's stiff dried out fur. "I found him in the woods. I wanted to show you guys what's gonna happen to the red fox those two guys are hunting."

"Now you showed us," Steve said. "Throw it back in the woods."

Boris laughed. "You're kidding. Arthur saved my life. I dove out a window, got up, started running, then, I tripped over something. I fell flat just as the barn blew up. Some big pieces of wood flew over right where I would have been if I was standing up. It was Arthur. He tripped me. He saved my life."

Boris petted the stiff dried out dead cat. "We're buddies now for life, right Arthur?"

Emil pointed at the dead cat. "If that dead cat answers you, I'm goin to Church again."

"Me too," Arnold said as he moved farther away from Boris and the dead cat.

Boris swung the dead cat back and forth. "Gotta give Arthur some air," he said.

"I told you guys that blast rattled his brain." Emil said.

Steve cocked his head. He listened for a moment. "I hear sirens coming this way."

Arnold got on his bike. "Fire engines. I'm leaving."

"Me too," Emil said as he followed Arnold out of the woods.

Steve jabbed a finger at Boris. "If you're taking that dead cat home, you stay way behind so nobody thinks you're with us."

"Yeah," Emil yelled back over his shoulder. "We don't want anyone thinking we're goofy as you."

Boris swung the dead cat around. "Oh yeah, me and Arthur will ride ahead so nobody thinks you're with us.

Boris passed the other boys. He rode down the highway swinging the dead cat around while yelling over and over, "Arthur's my cat. He used to be fat but somebody done squashed him flat."

The three boys slowed to let Boris get farther down the road.

"I told you guys he's nuts from that blast," Emil said.

"I think you're right," Arnold said.

Steve began pedaling faster. "Let's keep him in sight in case he flips out anymore and needs help."

Emil looked worried. "You think we should call somebody from the banana farm to come get him when we get back to the clubhouse."

Steve shook his head. "It's probably temporary. He'll get over it in a few days."

"Boy, I sure hope so," Emil said. "I'd hate to tell his Ma what happened.

Up ahead, Boris came to an intersection where a car was waiting to go through. He pulled up to the driver's side. Four white haired old ladies were in the car taking a drive out in the country. "It's a beautiful day for a lovely drive in the country," Boris said. The driver was startled for a moment, then, she smiled at Boris. "Yes it is. We just had a wonderful lunch and now we're enjoying a lovely ride through this beautiful countryside." She turned to the other ladies saying, "Such a nice polite young man."

Boris then screwed up his face in a frightening mass of rage. He held up the stiff dried out dead cat almost inside the driver's window dangling it inches from her face.

"If it's such a great day," he yelled at the startled women, "why did you run over and squash my cat?"

The white haired old lady took one look at the stiff dried out dead cat inches from her face. She let out a piercing shriek that people later said was heard two miles down the road. The white haired old lady sitting next to her leaned past the driver and saw the dead cat dangling in the window. Her shrieks were louder than the driver's.

The two white haired old ladies in the back seat stared at the dead cat Boris swung back and forth just outside the driver's window as he yelled, "You killed my cat, You ran over Arthur. You squashed him flat."

Their screams were louder than those coming from the two white haired old ladies sitting in the front seats. The panicked driver's feet slipped off the brake and the clutch at the same time. The car lurched through the intersection into a field where it stalled. The screaming and shrieking of the old ladies scared a bunch of cows grazing in the field. They ran to the far end of the field and huddled together at the fence.

Boris rode through the intersection and down the road swinging the stiff dried out dead cat while yelling, "You killed my cat. You squashed him flat. You killed my cat. You squashed him flat."

Emil, Arnold and Steve stopped before reaching the intersection.

"He's blown his top," Emil said.

"He's gone crazy," Arnold said.

"I don't believe it," Steve said.

Arnold pedaled away fast as he could. He yelled back to Steve and Emil. "I believe it. I'm getting out of here before the cops come."

"Should we help the old ladies?" Emil asked.

Steve shook his head. "Let's get away from here. They'll be Ok when they calm down. They can start up and drive out of there. It doesn't look they're stuck. Let's go before they realize we were with Boris."

Emil kept shaking his head as they rode home fast as they could. "I knew he was gonna be trouble when he came out of the woods with that dead cat."

Chapter 3

The next morning Boris was in the club waiting for the other boys. When they walked in, he was sitting at the table staring straight ahead humming and petting the stiff dried out dead cat in his lap.

"Hi Boris," each boy said as they came into the clubhouse. He never answered. He kept humming and petting the dead cat while staring straight ahead. Steve bent over close to his face. "Boris, Boris, are you in there?" He waved his hand in front of Boris's face the way he saw them do in the movies. Boris kept staring straight ahead humming and petting the stiff dried out dead cat in his lap. Emil and Arnold bent over. They looked into Boris's staring eyes. They waved their hands in front of his face. They called out his name over and over. There was no response as he kept staring and humming and petting the stiff dried out dead cat.

Steve motioned with a movement of his head for Emil and Arnold to follow him out of the clubhouse. Once outside, he took them away from the open front door.

"You think he's faking being goofy?" Arnold asked in a low voice.

Steve shook his head. "I don't know. I've never seen anyone go nuts."

Emil leaned over to glance into the clubhouse. "I think Boris is faking it just to get some attention. I remember last year in school, one of my teachers said people do that sometimes for no other reason just to get attention."

Steve thought about this. "You may be right Emil."

"How can we find out?" Arnold asked.

Steve glanced at the open door, then said in a low voice, "I read where a loud noise or saying something scary will snap a person out of what Boris is doing."

Emil grinned. "I know what to do. Watch."

Emil went to the clubhouse door. He looked in and yelled, "Run you guys. Here comes Bosco and Usual. They're looking for Boris."

A look of pure panic flashed over Boris's face. He opened his mouth but nothing came out. He looked one way then another for an escape route. He let out an anguished wail then dove under the table. "Tell em I'm innocent. Tell em I didn't do it. Tell em I went to Mexico."

Emil darted into the clubhouse. "Gotcha," he said. "You been fakin it."

"Fakin what?"

"Fakin you're nuts," Emil said.

Boris poked his head out from underneath the table. "Emil, that's a rotten trick to play on a buddy who almost got blown up."

Steve started into the clubhouse when he looked down the street. Bosco and Usual were still a block away. Their clothes were black with soot. They each had bandages on their heads and limped as they came toward the clubhouse.

"Uh, oh," Steve said darting into the clubhouse. "Here comes Bosco and Usual. They're probably heading up to Jimmy the Cheese's place."

Boris stood up. "I ain't fallin for that again." He went into a boxer's stance. He danced around throwing punches into the air. "Nobody scares Boris the Great, not even those two crooks Bosco and Usual."

Still using fancy footwork and throwing punches into the air, Boris moved backwards out of the clubhouse yelling, "Boris the Great will take em on one at a time or both together. We'll see how tough those guys are who want to shoot innocent little red foxes."

Steve, Emil and Arnold followed him out the door. They all pointed to the two men but Boris never got the warning in time.

Boris backed right into Bosco and Usual who were passing on the sidewalk.

"Watch where you're goin," Boris growled then did some fancy steps and punching moves as he turned to face Bosco and Usual. He stopped. He looked down at Bosco's big clodhopper shoes. His gaze moved up until he was looking into Bosco's grim face. He managed a weak grin.

"I'm, I'm sorry Sir," he said in a high squeaky voice.

Bosco grabbed him by the shirt front with one hand. He pulled him close and up until Boris was on his tip toes.

"Good thing you said you was sorry," Bosco growled into Boris's face. "Don't let it happen again." Boris saluted several times while saying in a voice that was now higher and squeakier "Yes Sir, I mean no Sir. It won't happen again Sir."

"It better not Fatso."

Bosco took a long look at Boris's face then at his bushy hair. "Ain't I seen you somewhere before?"

Boris shook his head. "No Sir, no Sir. I never leave here Sir."

Bosco let go of Boris's shirt. He pushed him back. Boris stumbled, got his balance then ran to his parent's grocery store saying as he went, "My Ma's calling me."

Bosco and Usual watched Boris go. "You think he looks like the guy at the farm, that bushy hair, big butt?"

Usual shook his head. "Naw, this one's too dumb looking to pull off something like that."

Bosco looked toward the store and shook his head as the two men continued up the street toward Jimmy's pool room.

Steve, Arnold and Emil went back into the clubhouse.

"Boy. That was close," Steve said as the boys sat down at the table.

Emil wiped the sweat from his brow. "We got to be real careful those guys can't connect or blame us for their barn blowing up."

"Yeah. I just ain't up to spending the next twenty five years in jail," Arnold said.

Chapter 4

Bosco and Usual limped down the stairs to Jimmy's pool room. They heaved big sighs as they sat down at a table where Jimmy was waiting for them. He regarded the two bandaged and singed men through clouds of cigar smoke.

"I talked to the Fire Chief about the fire and explosion," he said as he learned forward toward the two men. He shook his head. "How could anybody knock over two of my best men?"

"Ok," Jimmy said. "What happened? How'd somebody get the drop on you two guys?"

Usual put out both hands palm up. "We was ambushed Boss."

"Yeah." Bosco said. "We heard noises over at the chicken coops like a fox or something was bothering the hens."

"We grabbed our shotguns, went out to see what the trouble was," Usual added. "That's when they opened the coops up and shooed the chickens out at us."

"We couldn't see nothing with all them panicked chickens hopping everywhere, running around in circles, squawking and clucking . . ." Bosco's voice trailed off like he was remembering a bad dream.

Usual shuddered. "Then they hit us from behind. Ambushed us. Musta used clubs or something, knocked us down. Musta been ten or fifteen of em."

Bosco shook his head. "Nah, had to be twenty of em coming at us from every direction. We was outnumbered but we put up a good fight."

"Yeah, yeah." Usual said waving his arms. "We beat em off. We retreated toward the barn to guard the still, not let em near it."

"That's when they came at us with shotguns," Bosco said making motions like he had a shotgun at his shoulder.

"We was pinned down. They kept on shooting at us hitting lots of chickens, feathers flying everywhere," Usual said. "It was like in a snowstorm.

We couldn't see nothing." Bosco shook his head. "It was bad Boss, real bad. That's when that fat guy with the bushy hair wearing nothing but big, baggy underwear ran out of all those feathers yelling and blasting away with a shotgun."

"Jumped right over us like he was in the Olympics or something." Usual added. "We got off a couple of shots but couldn't see too good because of all the feathers. He was heading for the barn."

Jimmy nodded and puffed on his cigar as the two men went on with their story of the battle at the farm.

We were out of ammo but we still chased that bushy haired guy into the barn," Bosco said. Usual was more excited now. He waved his arms as he talked. "We figured he was going after the still. We ran after him but soon as we got in the door, the boiler exploded, blew us right out the door."

"What happened to the bushy haired guy?" Jimmy asked.

"He musta put a bomb or something on the still as he went by, then went out a window at the far end," Bosco said.

Usual shook his head. "We put up a good fight Boss but there was just too many of em for us."

There was a long silence while Jimmy drummed on the table with his finger tips. Bosco and Usual fidgeted in their chairs. They kept glancing at each other then at Jimmy as he puffed and drummed as he stared past them into the dark poolroom.

Without looking at either Bosco or Usual, he said, "You know what?"

"What?" Usual asked.

"What?" Bosco asked.

"Icepick, that's what," Jimmy said giving the two men a knowing look.

"Icepick?" Bosco said.

"Icepick?" Usual asked.

They looked at each other with puzzled expressions.

Usual shook his head as he stared at Jimmy. "But, but, Icepick's a skinny bald headed little punk from Goosetown."

"Yeah," Bosco added. "The guy we saw was fat with big bushy hair and wore big baggy underwear."

"You already told me that," Jimmy said. "He was the decoy, one of the gang. Icepick's too smart to show his face. You can bet he was back in the bushes directing the operation."

Usual had a puzzled expression on his face. "But, but, the last time we heard, Icepick was knocking over paperboys stealing their money and papers."

Jimmy gave them another knowing look. "I heard all about Icepick. I talked to Uncle Junie right after I heard about the explosion at the farm."

"Wow, you talked to Uncle Junie, the big Boss in Cleveland?" Usual said.

Usual turned to Bosco. He jerked a thumb toward Jimmy. "He talked to Uncle Junie, the big Boss in Cleveland.

"Are we gonna whack Icepick?" Bosco asked.

Jimmy shook his head. "We ain't whacking nobody."

"Why ain't we? He's the guy who tried to whack us," Bosco said.

"Because Uncle Junie is Icepick's Uncle and Uncle Junie wouldn't like it if we whacked his Sister's boy. That's why," Jimmy said.

Bosco and Usual just stared at Jimmy. Finally, Usual said, "This little shrimp tries to do us in and we ain't supposed to get even."

"That's right." Jimmy said. "Uncle Junie says he don't want that dummy nephew of his back in Cleveland so he gave him a pool room in Goosetown where he can make some book, keep him out of Uncle Junie's hair. He said Icepick may be trying to branch out into my turf. But Uncle Junie said not to worry. Icepick is so dumb the cops will get him real quick. Uncle Junie said he had to get him out of Cleveland. He didn't want him to get killed there with some of the dumb capers he dreamed up like when he got drunk one night, said he wanted to be the first Slovak Jesse James by holding up a train. Trouble was he picked a freight train. He was almost run over when he stood in the middle of the tracks waving a gun yelling 'Pull over. This is a stickup.'"

"Geez," Bosco said. "A guy dumb as that can give mobstering a bad name."

"Uncle Junie says keep an eye on him." Jimmy said. "He wants to know if he gets too far outta line, screws up business down here in Akron, then he says he's gotta do something, nephew or no nephew."

Usual looked puzzled. "You want we should go over to Goosetown to keep an eye on him?" Jimmy waved a hand at Usual. "Nah, I don't mean that. We ain't got no time to babysit him. You guys keep your eyes open for anything funny happening around here. Watch to see if he tries to hook up with some guys around here who'd like to see me back running numbers for Uncle Junie in Cleveland."

Usual held out both hands palms up toward Jimmy. "What you want us to do until you get another still at the farm and the barn rebuilt?"

"I got plenty of work around here for you guys. I want both of you to check all of our customers. See if anybody's been around trying to sell them their booze. Tell Bruno at the fireworks factory to be careful he don't let nobody in he don't know. Go over to Millie's. Tell her to look out for a skinny guy with a pillow under his shirt to make him look fat wearing a bushy haired wig."

Bosco grinned. "I'll go see Millie."

Jimmy shook his head. "Both you guys go. Shows everybody we mean business."

"Who else we should check?" Usual asked.

Jimmy nods. "Yeah, I almost forgot about Stronoff. And Yossitch. Tell them to watch for suspicious guys hanging around like somebody they don't know trying to buy hot stuff and booze. Icepick could be setting them up you tell them."

Jimmy looked at each man. He lit a new cigar bigger than the one he just stubbed out. "Any questions?"

Bosco shrugged. "Not from me."

"Me neither," Usual said.

Chapter 5

It was a beautiful Summer Sunday morning in Ohio. The streets were quiet as families ate breakfast and got ready for church. Arnold and Steve were in the clubhouse waiting for Boris and Emil. Emil left to get Boris. He came back a few minutes later.

"Boris Ma probably made him go to church with her. Mr. Choska's sitting on the back porch. He's either asleep or passed out. There's a jug of Jimmy the Cheese's bootleg whiskey by his chair. I tried to wake him up but he's out cold."

Steve and Arnold followed Emil to the back porch of the Choska's living quarters behind the family store. Steve went to where Mr. Choska sat slumped in the chair, his eyes closed, head back, his mouth open. His eye glasses askew. He was snoring and making odd grunting noises in between snores.

"At least he ain't dead," Steve said.

"Dead guys don't snore like that," Arnold said.

"Dead guys don't snore at all," Emil said.

Steve laughed. "Emil you are a master of the obvious."

Emil stood in front of Mr. Choska for a long moment, then said, "I got an idea. Let's have some fun with him."

Steve gave Emil a suspicious look. "What kind of fun."

"My dad told me about a guy down at the Hungarian Club who passed out from too much whiskey. They painted his glasses black. When he opened his eyes he thought he was blind. He began crying and wailing it was the booze that made him blind. Then he knocked off his glasses and yelled he could see again. He kept on yelling he was healed, claimed it was a miracle. My Dad said the guy never drank another drop after that."

"I don't Know Emil," Steve said shaking his head. "That's a pretty rough joke to play on a buddy's Dad."

"Aw c'mon Steve," Arnold said. "We all know Mr. Choska likes his whiskey."

"Yeah, Mrs. Choska is always screaming at him for sneaking down in the basement to nip at his home brew," Emil said.

"No wonder the guy sneaks around drinking in the basement with Mrs. Choska yelling at him and Boris all the time," Arnold said.

Steve thought for a moment. "Those two guys from the Jimmy the Cheese gang making him buy their bootleg whiskey sure hasn't helped by the looks of what happened to him today."

"See, what'd I just tell you about the guy at the Hungarian club who swore off drinking after they painted his glasses black and he thought he went blind," Emil said.

Arnold had a pious look on his face. "We'd be doing him, Mrs. Choska and Boris a big favor if we did the same thing to Mr. Choska and he swore off drinking."

Steve rubbed his chin for a moment as he thought about that. "Well, maybe you guys are right. Maybe it would help him."

Emil went into the tool shed. He came out with a can of black paint, a small brush, a hammer and some nails. Steve looked puzzled. "What you doing with that hammer and nails?"

"You'll see," Emil said grinning.

Arnold took the can of paint and brush. He straightened Mr. Choska's glasses then proceeded to paint the lenses black.

Steve looked at the painted lenses. He had a worried expression on his face when he glanced up at Arnold and Emil. "Can he get that paint off" Will it ruin his glasses?"

"Nah," Emil said. "It's the kind of paint they use to put signs on the windows. It'll wash right off."

Emil held up the hammer. "Now for the master touch." He pointed to Mr. Choska's shoes. "You guys unlace them, lift his feet out real gentle."

Steve and Arnold unlaced and took off Mr. Choska's shoes. Steve pointed to the hammer Emil held. "You start hammering, you'll wake him up."

Emil grinned. "It'll take an earthquake to wake him after he drank Jimmy Cheese's lousy bootleg whiskey."

Emil tapped the nails into the inside of Mr. Choska's tenner shoes securing them to the floor of the porch.

"Ok, now all we have to do is go across the street, wait for Boris and Mrs. Choska to get home from church," Emil said. "She sees him passed out on the porch, she'll start yelling at him from thirty feet away loud enough to wake him up."

The three boys walked across the street, found a shady spot under a big tree and waited.

"Church should be out any time now," Arnold said.

Within a few minutes the church bells signaled the end of the services.

"Here they come," Emil said with a slight motion of his head down the street to where Mrs. Choska and Boris were walking toward the corner. Mrs. Choska saw her husband slumped in a chair on the back porch with the jug of bootleg whiskey beside him.

"Choska," she screamed in a voice loud enough to freeze some of the congregation still in their seats, others on the steps, in the parking lot and on the sidewalk. Her screams grew louder as she ran toward her passed out husband.

Mr. Choska stirred. He twisted around in his chair. He grunted. He groaned.

"He's waking up," Arnold said.

Mr. Choska turned his head from side to side.

"He's trying to see," Steve said.

The screaming Mrs. Choska, followed by a wide eyed Boris, reached the porch. The startled Mr. Choska gripped the arms of his chair. He let out a yowl that almost, but not quite, drowned out his wife's yelling and screaming.

He began yelling, "I can't see. I can't see. I'm blind." He struggled to his feet. He tried to take a step. His nailed down shoes wouldn't move." "I can't walk. I can't move my feet. I'm paralyzed." He stretched out his arms. "Help me. Somebody help me. I can't see. I'm blind. I can't walk. I'm paralyzed."

Hearing this, Mrs. Choska stopped running. She stopped screaming. She gaped at the sight of her husband standing on the porch wailing, waving his arms around and trying to lift his feet off the floor. Mrs. Choska fell to her knees in front of the porch. "Ohhh Dear Lord," she said in a pleading voice clasping her hands in prayer, "Save that no-good boozing bum who spends Sunday morning drinking and don't go to church with his God fearing wife and his dear little boy who I got right beside me on his knees praying for his drunken Father." Mrs. Choska reaches up, grabs Boris arms and pulls him down beside her. "Get on your knees, start praying."

Boris put his hands together in prayer. Bewildered, Boris let go with the only prayer he knew by heart, "Dear Lord, we thank you for this food." Mrs. Choska smacked him on the shoulder saying, "Not that one. That's for supper." Then she thought better of having Boris pray anymore so she said, "Run, go get Rev. Shushnic. We need help driving that whiskey devil out of your Pa."

Panicked by the frenzied wailing of his Father and the loud praying of his Mother, Boris ran to the church to get Reverend Shushnic. In between her screeching and yelling he heard his Mother praying, "Ohhh Dear Lord, save that sinner Choska's soul from demon rum. Let him see again so he can work in the produce department picking out the bad stuff."

Four neighborhood women on the way home from church heard the yelling and praying coming from behind Choska's store. They were stunned at the sight of Mrs. Choska on her knees by the porch praying for the Good Lord to make her drunken bum of a husband see and walk again. They saw Mr. Choska on the porch waving his arms toward the Heavens praying and yelling about the injustice of it all for him being struck blind and paralyzed for having a few relaxing drinks on Sunday.

"Choska's been boozing again." one of the women said.

Mrs. Choska looked at the women. She waved her arm toward the hapless Mr. Choska. "Look at him," she yelled. "Choska's been struck blind. He's paralyzed from drinking that Jimmy the Cheese's lousy rotten bootleg whiskey."

"I knew it, I knew it," one woman said. "That Choskas been at it again."

"We gotta help that poor Mrs. Choska," another woman said. The four women fell to their knees beside Mrs. Choska who yelled to them, "Pray, pray for Choska's immortal soul."

The four women began praying loud, then, louder as each tried to drown out the other and all them together came close to drowning out Mrs. Choska as well as Mr. Choska's frenzied wailing, yelling and praying.

Boris was back in a few minutes followed by a wide eyed and puffing Reverend Shushnic who sized up the situation right away after seeing the jug of bootleg whiskey on the porch. The good Reverend had a grim determined half smile on his face thankful he had this chance to battle for a parishioner's soul against the forces of evil that lead a man to drink. When he got to the Choska's back porch, the Reverend Shushnic took one look at a weeping, wailing, ranting and raging Mr. Choska waving his arms around as he yelled. He saw the kneeling women and Mrs. Choska trying to out do each other with their pleas for Mr. Choska's salvation. At that point, the good Reverend Shushnic realized he hit the jackpot for a no-holds battle with the dark forces of evil for the soul of one of his flock. He fell to his knees beside Mrs. Choska. She turned to him with both hands clenched tight.

"Do something Reverend Shushnic. Do something to save my poor husband from a life of darkness where he can't work in the store anymore."

Reverend Shushnic rolled up his sleeves. He spit on both hands like he was going to saw wood or dig a ditch. "I'll pray for a miracle," he yelled above the din of Mr. Choska yelling, Mrs. Choska calling on all Angels in Heaven to help her poor husband and the loud praying of the four women who had joined the fight to save Mr. Choska's soul.

The good Reverend Sushnic went into the battle against demon rum man by praying so loud people later claimed they heard him all the way over at Anders Street which was at least a quarter mile away. His deep voice rose and fell as he implored the Good Lord to drive out the demons that possessed Mr. Choska that led him to a life of boozing. It was later said that some of the men in the neighborhood who snuck around to the two beer joints in the neighborhood swore off drinking, after hearing Reverend Shushnics battle with the evil forces that lead a man to a life of drinking bootleg whiskey.

Scared and more bewildered than ever, Boris dropped to his knees beside his Mother, put his hands together and began praying in a loud voice, "Now I lay me down to sleep . . ." He broke it off when he saw the Reverend Sushnic giving him a puzzled look.

Steve, Arnold and Emil watched from across the street.

"Wow," Arnold said. "This is better'n watching the Three Stooges."

Steve shook his head. "If this is what whiskey does, I'm never drinking a drop."

"Me neither," Emil said.

Mr. Choska's voice drowned out all the others as he made a thunderous plea waving his arms as he shouted, "Heal me Lord. I'll never touch that lousy stuff from Jimmy the Cheese again."

"Heal the drunken bum." Mrs. Choska yelled.

The Reverend Shushnic gave Mrs. Choska a surprised look. He shrugged. He let go with a thunderous, "Heal, heal the drunken bum."

Curious neighbors hearing the shouts and yelling and screaming and praying hurried to the Choska store and joined in with mighty choruses of "Heal, heal the drunken bum."

Caught up and energized by all the praying and shouting of so many people pulling for him, Mr. Choska stood. He gave a mighty heave trying to lift his right foot and take a step. To his amazement, his shoe pulled free. He took a step. He pulled hard on the other foot. The shoe came free. He lost his balance for a moment. His glasses fell off. Now, free of the black painted glasses, he looked around bewildered and confused. Then it hit him. He could see again. He could move his legs. He was no longer blind. He wasn't paralyzed anymore. He began dancing around on the porch pumping the air with both arms and yelling, "I can see. I can walk. I'm cured. It's a miracle."

The people on their knees were stunned at the sight of Mr. Choska dancing around on the porch. Their jaws dropped open. They couldn't say anything as they stared in amazement at the miracle they were witnessing. They watched Mr. Choska dance a jig then kick the jug of bootleg whiskey off the porch. "I'm healed, I'm healed. I can see. I can walk. I can dance. It's a miracle. It's a miracle," he yelled as he executed a nifty buck and a wing step.

Reverend Shushnic jumped to his feet. He pumped both arms in the air as he danced around yelling, "It's a miracle, it's a miracle. The drunken bum is healed."

The stunned crowd all jumped to their feet. They danced around waving their arms joining with Reverend Shusnic in yelling, "It's a miracle, it's a miracle, The drunken bum can see. The drunken bum can walk."

Mr. Choska picked up his glasses. His thumb rubbed off some of the paint. He sat down in his chair. He took off one shoe. He saw the two nails sticking out of the sole. He took off his other shoe and saw another two nails sticking out of that sole.

Everyone became quiet as they watched Mr. Choska rub the paint off his eyeglass lenses and examine his shoes and finding nails in them. They crowded around the back porch as Mr. Choska explained what happened. The four ladies who were first on the scene watched, shook their heads, and clucked.

Reverend Shushnic was disappointed. He shook his head. "We had a miracle going here for awhile. Now we got nothing." He stood. He kept shaking his head. His shoulders slumped. He walked back to the church shaking his head.

Mrs. Choska stood with her hands on her hips. "Who would do such a thing nailing a man's shoes to the floor so he couldn't move, painting his glasses black so he couldn't see?"

Chapter 6

Jimmy the Cheese, Bosco and Usual drove to the corner as the crowd milled around Choska's back porch. Jimmy tapped Bosco on the shoulder. "Stop, I want to see what's going on over here." They got out of the car. "What's happening here?" Jimmy asked two men watching.

One man stared at Jimmy for a moment, then said, "Ol man Choska got all likkered up on bad booze some new guy around here named Jimmy the Cheese sold him."

"Yeah," the other man said. "Then somebody painted his glasses black. Made him go crazy thinking he was blind as a bat."

"Not only that," the first man said, "They nailed his shoes to the porch so he couldn't lift his feet, made him think he was paralyzed."

The second man shook his head, "There oughta be a law against selling rotten whiskey to God fearing people, makes em pass out, go crazy thinking they're blind, can't walk."

"Yeah, there oughta be a law," the first man said.

"I hope they catch those guys who painted his glasses black, nailed his shoes to the porch," added the other man.

Bosco and Usual glanced at Jimmy who had a stunned look on his face. They followed him to the car. The two men watched them get in the car and drive off.

The first man gestured toward the car screeching tires as it roared away, leaving a trail of blue smoke. "You think they could be those new guys selling that lousy booze around here?"

The other man shook his head. "Naw, they look too dumb to be bootleggers."

Back at Jimmy's pool room the three men sat not saying anything. Usual glanced at Bosco who shrugged, "Whadda ya think Boss?"

Jimmy lit a cigar. He took a couple of puffs. He jabbed a finger at the two men sitting across from him. "You guys want to know what I think" I'll tell you what I think."

Bosco and Usual leaned toward Jimmy. "Yeah Boss, tell us what you think," Usual said.

Jimmy made an impatient gesture. "I'm getting to that."

"Yeah, yeah," Bosco said. We want to hear what you think Boss cause you don't think too much."

Usual kicked Bosco under the table.

"Ow," Bosco said. "What'd you kick me for?"

Jimmy smacked the table. "If you guys'll shut up for a minute, I'll tell you what I think."

He leaned toward the two men. He gave them a knowing look as he nodded. He paused then said, "I think one thing, Icepick."

Bosco and Usual looked at each other then said at the same time, "Icepick?"

Usual looked puzzled. "What about Icepick?"

"He set me up," Jimmy said. "That's what he did. He set me up."

Bosco looked puzzled. "How'd he do that?"

A cunning look flashed over Jimmy's face. "I got it all figured out. He put something in the booze to make Choska pass out, painted his glasses black so he'd think he was blind from drinking my stuff. That ain't enough for the crooked Icepick who don't play fair in this mobster business. He nails Choska's shoes to the porch so he can't walk. Now, Choska comes out of it from his old lady yelling at him. He opens his eyes. He can't see with his glasses painted black so he thinks he's blind. He can't lift his feet so now he figures he's paralyzed. He's yelling and hollering my stuff made him go blind, paralyzed him. Now, everybody around here thinks my stuff is so bad it'll paralyze them, make em go blind."

Bosco shook his head. "What a dirty rotten crook that Icepick is."

Chapter 7

The next morning Emil, Arnold and Steve were in the clubhouse.

Steve looked out the window. "Uh, oh, here comes Boris."

Arnold glanced out. "Looks like he ain't too happy. He musta figured out what we did."

"So what," Emil said. "We cured Mr. Choska's drinking problem."

"You're right," Steve said.

"We did our good deed for the day," Emil added.

Boris came in the clubhouse. "That was a dirty rotten trick you guys pulled on my Dad."

"We cured your Dad's drinking problem," Steve said.

Boris thought for a moment. "Yeah. I guess you did." He looked around. "What you guys doin?"

"We're having a meeting," Steve said.

"About what?"

"Saving that little red fox from those two guys who want to shoot it," Steve said.

Arnold shook his head. "We're just four kids. How we stopping two of Jimmy the Cheese's gang who got shotguns?"

"We'll get to the fox before those two guys do, get him out of the woods, take him somewhere else where he'll be safe," Steve said.

"And how we doing that?" Emil asked. We just walk up to the fox telling him he got to come with us so he doesn't get his butt shot off?"

"Boy, Emil, you are one real dummy," Boris said. "We trap it, that's how we get it out of the woods."

"We don't have any traps," Arnold said.

"We buy one," Boris said.

Emil shook his head. "And you called me a dummy. Where we getting the money to buy a trap?"

"I'm working on it," Steve said as he opened a book lying on the table beside him. He held it up.

"We don't have to buy a trap. We make one just like it shows how in this book." He held it up for the others to see the title. "I got it at the library."

"Trapping Wild Animals," Arnold read.

Steve opened to a page he had marked. He pointed to an illustration.

"A big hole in the ground," Boris said.

"Yeah," Steve said. "We dig a big hole, cover it with leaves. We put some bait on top of the leaves and . . . ."

"And we got him," Arnold added.

"What we using for bait?" Emil asked.

"I'll get some scraps my Dad trims off the meat and throws away," Boris said.

"Ok, we start tomorrow," Steve said. "We meet here first thing in the morning. Emil, you and Arnold bring shovels. Boris brings the bait. I'll bring a pick."

The next morning the four boys met at the clubhouse. They rode their bikes to the pond where they'd last seen the fox. Steve looked around then pointed to the path almost hidden by bushes.

"The fox ran out of there and grabbed Boris's lunch. We'll dig the trap right on the path that goes back in the bushes."

Emil, Arnold and Steve lay in the shade when it was Boris's turn to dig. After awhile, his muffled voice came from the hole. "Hey you guys, it's somebody else's turn to dig. I'm tired."

"I'll check it," Arnold said getting up and going over to the site of the trap where several mounds of dirt was piled around it. He looked down into the hole. "Where you digging to . . . China?" he said to Boris.

"You guys said you wanted it deep enough so the fox couldn't get out," Boris said.

Emil and Steve were now at the trap looking down at Boris.

"We're not trying to trap an elephant," Steve said as Arnold and Emil took hold of Boris's hands, pulling him up out of the hole. Boris ran over to the pond. He jumped in with his clothes still on. He swam around for awhile, then he took off his shirt and pants and threw them up on the bank. He climbed out of the pond wearing only his wet baggy underwear and tenner shoes. He spread his clothes out on a bush to dry along with the other boy's clothes. He took off his wet shoes and socks and set them out in the sun. He lad down under the shade of a big tree. "Ok, I did my share, you guys finish the trap."

The other boys gathered small branches and leaves they spread over the open hole. When they finished, Steve carefully laid the scraps of meat over top of the brush covering the trap.

"Ok," Steve said. "That should do it. The fox will smell the meat. He'll come after it real quick so we should leave here. We don't want to scare him away before he goes after the bait."

Arnold nodded. "Let's go to the farmhouse, see what those two guys are doing."

The boys hurried to the old farmhouse. They hid in the bushes just beyond the barnyard. Steve parted the branches for a better look.

"You guys ain't gonna believe this," he whispered. "Those guys got another still working. Take a look." The other boys pulled the bushes apart and looked across to where the barn had been. Several workmen were finishing a building with the still inside.

"Those guys really work fast," Arnold whispered.

A heavy set man wearing a white fedora hat and smoking a big cigar came out of the farmhouse.

"Jimmy the Cheese," Steve whispered.

The man stopped. He looked around. "Where are those two screw ups?" he asked one of the workmen. The man pointed to the woods. "They took shotguns, said they were heading toward the pond where they saw that chicken stealing fox. Said they were getting it this time."

The four boys looked at each other. Steve motioned for them to be quiet and follow him. They moved through the heavy bushes without making a sound. When they were far enough away so they wouldn't be heard they stopped.

"If that fox fell in the trap those guys will shoot it right there," Steve said.

The four boys hurried through the woods until they came within sight of the pond. They moved down the path until they could see the trap. The leaves and branches covering it were gone.

"We got it," Emil whispered. "We got the red fox."

"What do we do now?" Arnold asked.

Steve took a sack out of his pocket. "We stick the fox in here then take him to another woods where he'll be safe from those two crooks."

The four boys moved toward the hole. Steve held up a hand motioning the others to stop. He listened, then a puzzled look flashed over his face.

"What, what?" Boris asked.

Steve put a finger to his lips. "You guys hear something?"

Muffled noises were coming from the hole. The boys crept closer staying in the cover of the bushes.

"You thinking what I'm thinking?" Steve whispered.

"Yeah," Emil said.

Arnold cupped a hand to an ear. "Bosco and Usual. We got Bosco and Usual."

Boris had a terrified look on his face. "You mean, you mean we trapped Bosco and Usual in that hole?"

"We did unless a fox can talk," Emil whispered.

Just then Bosco's and Usual's mud covered heads popped up out of the hole.

Boris gasped. "We're dead. They'll kill us. They'll murderize us." He let out a loud wail. He jumped up from their hiding place. He ran through the dense vegetation, down the path toward the trap. He hurdled the two surprised men who ducked back in the hole as the panicked Boris sailed over them yelling, "Murder, murder." He hit the ground running then disappeared in the bushes.

Bosco came up out of the hole wiping mud from his face. "It's him," he yelled. "It's Icepick Pete."

Usual came up scraping mud from his face. "Where, where?"

Bosco pointed to the woods. "He went that way. Give me my shotgun."

Bosco grabbed his shotgun from Usual. He let go with both barrels into the woods. Usual ducked back in the hole. He came up with his shotgun and fired both barrels in the same direction.

"Time to go," Steve said as he headed toward the pond where they hid their bicycles. Emil and Arnold were right behind him. They heard the shotgun blasts as Bosco and Usual fired wildly into the woods.

When the three boys got to the main road, they saw Boris way ahead pedaling like he was heading for the finish line in an Olympic bike race. They hurried to the clubhouse but Boris wasn't there.

Chapter 8

Bosco and Usual went down the stairs into Jimmy's poolroom. Jimmy was busy studying the racing form. Jocko was at the counter. He looked at the two men, then laughed. "Hey Jimmy," he said. "Look at these two mud babies. They musta been out making mud pies."

Bosco grabbed the skinny man by the shirt front. He dragged him halfway across the counter.

"You're a funny guy, Jocko, a real funny guy. You'll be even funnier when I break your scrawny neck."

"I was just kidding Bosco," he gasped. "I didn't mean nothing by it."

Jimmy jumped out of his chair. He grabbed Bosco's arm. "Let him go Bosco. You're breaking his neck."

Bosco let go of Jocko's shirt front. He pushed him back. "Next time you're just kidding around, I'll finish the job."

Jimmy pulled Jocko back to his desk where he sat down rubbing his neck.

"You guys cut it out. We got other problems to worry about." He looked at Bosco and Usual who were still covered with mud. "Awright. What happened to you guys?"

Bosco flicked some mud off his forehead. "We was ambushed out in the woods when we was hunting for the fox."

Usual spit some mud out on the floor. "Musta been ten guys jumped us from behind."

Bosco nodded. "Maybe even fifteen. They tried to bury us right there in the woods. Shoved us into this hole they dug." Bosco said.

Jimmy eyed both men with a skeptical look. "What then?"

"When they saw we had shotguns, they ran," Bosco said.

"You get a look at any of them?" Jimmy asked.

Usual nodded. "Yeah, we saw one of them. It was that bushy haired fat guy Icepick Pete again."

Bosco waved his arms. "He came out of the bushes right at us screaming his head off he was gonna murder us."

"Yeah, he was yelling and hollering like some kind of wild crazy man." Usual said.

"When he saw we was trying to get the mud off our shotguns, he jumped right over top of us, ran into the woods with his gang right behind him," Bosco added.

Usual shuddered. "He was a wild man, a crazy man."

"Yeah, yeah, yeah," Bosco added. "He ran so fast we couldn't get a shot at him before he went in the bushes."

Jimmy puffed on his cigar as he looked past the two men. He nodded. "Icepick again, huh? The same guy who blew up my barn and still. Now it looks like he's got a gang with him. This is getting serious. I'm talking to Uncle Junie. He's got to do something about that guy before he kills you guys and runs me out of business."

Chapter 9

Emil, Arnold and Steve were back in the clubhouse. Steve went to the door. He looked out.

"See him yet?" Emil asked.

"Not yet."

"He's probably still running, halfway to Cleveland by now," Arnold said.

"For a guy who talks so tough, he sure does panic," Emil said.

Boris pops up in the open window. "I heard that. I just hid here so I could hear what you guys are saying about me." He came around through the front door. "Hah, you guys thought I was scared. I just wanted to scare those two crooks so they wouldn't get a good shot at you."

"Yeah, yeah sure," Emil said. "You weren't scared at all. That's why you set a new record running and jumping over those guys in the hole."

Boris sat at the table. He pulled out a candy bar. He looked around real quick saying, "No dibs," then but off half of it. He held the candy bar out to the others. "Ok, Ok, you guys can have dibs," he said spraying little pieces of candy onto the table. The three boys pushed back away from the table and the spraying pieces of candy.

"Boris, you're a slob," Emil said.

"Don't talk with your mouth full," Arnold said. "And don't spray that stuff all over the table."

"Gee, my buddies don't want dibs, I'll just eat it all." He stuffed the rest of the candy bar in his mouth then wiped the crumbs off the table with the sleeve of his shirt. "There," he said, "Now you happy Arnold?"

"You just sprayed more crumbs out on the table," Arnold said.

Boris swiped his arm across the table cleaning off the new batch.

Steve sat back with his arms folded, watching. "You guys sitting here arguing all day or we getting back to saving the red fox?"

"We might as well sit here and argue. We ain't having much luck trying to trap that fox," Emil said.

"I got another idea," Steve said as he opened a book lying on the table in front of him.

Boris got up. "Hah, the genius got another idea. I'm going home so I don't get killed for good this time."

"What now?" Emil asked.

Arnold shook his head. "Why don't you guys let him finish instead of always making remarks."

"Thanks Arnold," Steve said. He held up the book. "This is that book on trapping animals." He pointed to a page in the open book. "It says here, this is a trap that never misses." He turned the book around to show the other boys a drawing of a spring trap made out of a bent over sapling. The other boys studied the drawings while Steve read the directions on how to make the trap.

"You guys want to do it?" he asked.

They all agreed to go out right after lunch and set the new spring trap.

"We need a hatchet to cut the trees and some rope," Steve said.

"I'll bring my Boy Scout hatchet and some more bait," Boris said.

Emil smacked Boris on the shoulder. "You never was no boy scout."

"Ow, cut that out," Boris said smacking Emil back. "I wanted to be one anyway."

Chapter 10

The boys rode their bikes out to near the pond and hid them in the dense brush. They went back to the first trap they had dug in the path and covered it over with small branches and leaves then put a piece of meat on top.

"We might as well keep this trap just in case the fox comes by here again," Steve said.

The boys went up the trail away from the pond and the first trap looking for a young tree they could bend over. They found one and began making their trap. Emil climbed up the tree. He tied a rope near the top then joined the other three boys in pulling the rope bending the tree down.

"Emil, you and Boris hold the tree down while me and Arnold will get some pieces of wood for the trap's trigger," Steve said.

"Hey Boris, where'd you leave the bait?" Arnold asked.

Boris turned. He let go of the tree as he looked around at Arnold. The tree snapped upright taking Emil with it. He let out a long yell as he swung up.

"What you let go for you dummy," he yelled at Boris.

"You sounded just like Tarzan," Boris said. "You oughta be in the movies."

Steve came back to where Boris was standing looking up at the swaying Emil. "Will you guys shut up. If there was a fox around he'd be a mile away by now."

Emil climbed down the tree. "I could'a been killed because of you," he yelled at Boris.

"You weren't so let's get this thing done," Arnold said.

They bent the tree down again and held it while Steve set the bait inside the loop of rope on the ground. He pounded a stake through the meat so that if the fox pulled on the meat it would loosen the rope and let the tree swing upright trapping the fox in the loop of the rope. Steve motioned the other boys back away from the trap. "Be careful you don't step in here or you'll be hanging upside down swinging in the breeze."

"This is hot work," Boris said.

"Yeah, let's go swimming for awhile, then we can come back to check the trap," Arnold said.

"We can't stay too long," Steve said. "If we catch the fox we don't want to let him hang there."

The boys went over to the pond and swam for awhile. While they were dressing Steve looked up. He cupped one ear and listened.

"What?" Boris asked.

"I thought I heard something," Steve said.

"So did I," Arnold said.

"Maybe it was the fox making noises after getting caught in the trap," Emil added.

Steve started running up the path toward the trap. "Let's go." When they got close to the trap, Steve motioned them to hold up and be quiet. He stepped off the path into the bushes. He listened then motioned the others to follow. The sounds coming from the trap were louder.

"Don't sound like no fox to me," Arnold whispered.

Steve parted the bushes. "Oh, oh," he said.

Boris looked. "It's Usual," he whispered.

The short fat man dangled from the rope trap by one ankle, his hands not touching the ground. He was grunting and gurgling while he tried to pull himself up and grab hold of the rope. Just then, the boys heard Bosco yelling from somewhere in the woods. "Hey, Usual, where are you?"

"I'm hanging from a tree. Get me down."

Bosco came crashing through the woods. He stopped when he saw Usual dangling on the rope. He pushed his hat back and leaned on his shotgun. "What you hanging around here for? I thought you was chasing the red fox." He bent over laughing. "You hear that Usual? You're hanging around here."

"Get me down," Usual gurgled.

Bosco pulled a pocketknife from his pocket. He cut the rope holding Usual's ankle. When the rope separated, Usual fell to the ground. He lay there for a long moment, then yelled at Bosco, "Not like that you dummy. I could'a been killed."

"You said to cut you down," Bosco said.

Usual sat up rubbing his shoulder and ankle. "Yeah, but I didn't say to kill me while you was doing it."

The boys in the bushes were watching not daring to move or make a sound. Boris had a scared look on his face. He backed away from the other boys, stepping on twigs and branches.

"What was that?" Bosco said as he brought up his shotgun.

"What was what?" Usual asked looking toward the bushes where the boys were hidden. He picked up his shotgun.

Boris panicked. "I'm getting out of here." He burst through the bushes and ran past Bosco and Usual yelling, "They're gonna murderize us," then disappeared in the bushes.

"It's him. It's Icepick Pete," Bosco yelled throwing the shotgun to his shoulder. He blasted both barrels at the bushes. Usual grabbed his shotgun. He rolled over onto his stomach and let go with both barrels.

Chapter 11

Bosco and Usual went into Jimmy's poolroom. Usual limped to a chair and sat with a loud sigh. Jocko looked up from counting and tallying betting sheets on a calculator. He looked up as Bosco and Usual came in. "Well if it ain't the two ace mobsters again."

Bosco reached over the counter after him. Jocko put his hands up in defense saying, "Geez, Bosco, can't you take a joke?" as he backed away.

"Yeah, I can take a joke but can you take this fist," Bosco made another grab across the counter at Jocko who backed farther away.

Jimmy the Cheese came out of the back room. "What's going on out here?"

"Me and Bosco was just horsing around . . . . Right Bosco?" Bosco shrugged his shoulders. Jimmy looked to where Usual sat rubbing his ankle.

"What's wrong with you?"

Usual just shook his head.

"Icepick Pete," Bosco said.

"That guy again?" Jimmy threw his hands up. "What now?"

Usual groaned as he went on rubbing his ankle.

Jimmy leaned over the counter to get a better look at Usual's ankle. "What'd Icepick do this time, kick you in the ankle?"

He turned to Jocko who by now was well back from the counter out of Bosco's reach.

"You hear that Jocko? Icepick kicked him in the ankle. That's funny stuff."

"Yeah Jimmy, that's funny stuff." Jocko shook his head as he went back to his calculator.

Jimmy turned to Bosco and Usual. "What happened this time?"

Usual groaned as he rubbed his sore ankle. "Icepick trapped me."

"Trapped you? How?"

Usual rubbed his ankle and moaned a few more times. "They had us surrounded, ran us into this trap on the path where I must have hit something with my foot. The next thing I know I'm hanging from a rope upside down."

"Yeah, yeah," Bosco said. "Soon as I saw Usual go up, I hit the ground, got off a couple of shots, scared them away. I figured they was coming through the bushes to finish off Usual."

"Yeah," Usual said. "I heard em coming. Must a been ten of em."

"More like twenty," Bosco added. "I didn't hit anyone but my shots scared em off."

Jimmy put both hands on the edge of the counter. He puffed harder and faster than ever as he gripped the wood. He looked at Bosco. "Did you see that bushy haired fat guy again?"

"Yeah. He went right past us, took a shot at Usual and me, missed, then ran in the bushes where the rest of his gang was hiding. I heard him yelling orders to the other guys. It was the same voice. I'd know it anywhere now."

Jimmy thought for a long time. "I got to talk to Uncle Junie about that guy. Looks like he ain't stopping till he scares us outta town." He banged his fist on the counter. "Uncle Junie gave me this territory. No goofy little punk is scaring me out of it even if he is Uncle Junie's nephew."

"What we doin about it Boss?" Usual asked then groaned as he rubbed his sore ankle.

"First, you guys check around with some of our customers. Find out if Icepick been around trying to get their business. Sell some more whiskey to Choska. We got to get people buying our stuff again."

Bosco walked and Usual limped as they made the rounds of some of the small businesses that Jimmy forced to buy his bootleg whiskey and scrawny chickens.

"Let's hit Choska last," Bosco said.

Usual limped along trying to keep up with the bigger man as they walked to Choska's store. The four boys were sitting on the big yellow milk bottle foxes in the shade of the store building. Arnold was the first to see them. "Uh, oh, look who's coming."

Boris took one look, and jumped off the box. "My Ma's calling." He ran inside the store.

"Don't look at them," Steve whispered as the two men approached the side door of the store. They stopped and stared at the three boys who never looked at them. Bosco jerked a thumb toward them. "Goofy looking bunch."

Usual grunted. "Yeah, the goofiest looking one is that fat kid with the bushy hair." The two men looked at each other. "Fat kid, bushy hair," Bosco said.

Usual shook his head. "Nah, I know what you're thinking. That kid looks too dumb to be a crook like Icepick Pete."

Bosco nodded. "Yeah, you got to have some smarts to be a mobster."

The two men went into the store. Bosco looked around. He saw Boris putting cans of food up on the shelves. He nudged Usual. "There's the fat one with the bushy hair."

Usual looked over at Boris. "Nah, like I just told you, he looks too dumb to be a crook like Icepick."

Mr. and Mrs. Choska were behind the counter when the two men came in. "It's trouble," Mr. Choska whispered. "They work for that guy Jimmy the Cheese who made me buy bootleg whiskey and his scrawny chickens."

Mrs. Choska folded her arms over her ample breasts. "You go in the back room, get some potatoes, I'll handle these crooks."

Mr. Choska scurried into the back room as the two men came up to the counter. Mrs. Choska gave each of them a cold eyed stare. "Can I help you gentlemen?"

Bosco gave her what he considered to be a smile. "Yeah, where's Choska. We wanna talk to him."

Mrs. Choska continued her defiant stance and stare. "He's sick. He can't come out here. He's sick from that lousy cheap no good whiskey that no good crook Jimmy the Cheese made him buy. So we ain't buying no more of his poison if that's what you're here for."

Bosco gave back her hard look. "If you ain't buying whiskey from us, who you buying it from?"

Usual pointed at the woman "Yeah, maybe you're doing business with a guy named Icepick Pete."

Mrs. Choska shifted her gaze to Usual. "I don't know no Icepick or whoever. I ain't buying no more of your cheap rotgut whiskey that almost killed my husband, almost made him blind and paralyzed. Now you two get out of my store before I call the cops."

Usual jabbed a finger toward Mrs. Choska. "Now, you listen to us lady if you know what's good for you or . . ."

Before Usual could finish Bosco grabbed him by the arm pulling him away from the counter. "Shut up," he whispered.

He held out both hands palms up in a gesture of what, what. "He didn't mean nothing. Sometimes he don't talk too good. He was just trying to ask you what's good today."

Mrs. Choska had her hands on her hips. "I knew exactly what he was saying. Now you two bums get out of my store or I call the cops and have you arrested for bootlegging and threatening me."

Bosco grinned. "Now, now, Mrs. Choska. We just came in to buy some of your fine groceries." He picked up a jar of pickles. "Like these pickles." He dropped the jar. "Oops, sorry Mrs. Choska. I sure am clumsy." He took a jar of mustard off the shelf. "We need some mustard for our hot dogs." He let the jar of mustard fall. It smashed on the floor with the pickles. "My gosh," Mrs. Choska. I got a bad case of the dropsies."

Usual took a jar of spaghetti sauce off a shelf. "We need some sauce if we're making spaghetti." He held out the jar to Bosco then dropped it. "Oops, sorry Mrs. Choska, I'm about as clumsy as Bosco."

Bosco took a big jar of jelly off the shelf. He held it out as though he was going to drop it. "We might even take this jelly too." He let go of it then caught the jar before it hit the floor. "Now, Mrs. Choska, do you think we can do some business?"

Mrs. Choska came from behind the counter. She grabbed the jar of jelly from Bosco. "All right, all right. I get your message. Bring me one jug of your rotten stuff."

Bosco took out a pad and pencil. He wrote, "That's a nice order Mrs. Choska, two jugs."

"I only ordered one."

Bosco turned to Usual. "Didn't she say she wanted two jugs of our fine product?"

Usual grinned, "Yeah, I heard her say it."

Mrs. Choska gripped the counter so hard her knuckles were white. She let out a long sigh. Her shoulders slumped. "All right, all right, give me two," she said in a small resigned tone of voice.

Bosco tore off a sheet from the pad and laid it on the counter. "That's four dollars Mrs. Choska."

She looked up. "I'll pay when you bring me the stuff."

Bosco shook his head. "Oh no, it's cash in advance. That's how Mr. Roman keeps his prices down. You know, no bookkeeping, that kind of stuff."

Mrs. Choska gave him a defiant look. She folded her arms across her chest. "I don't pay until I get my stuff, not before."

Bosco turned to the shorter man. "You know Usual, I think we could use a watermelon. He went to the produce shelf and picked up one. "This baby looks real good." He held it up like he was going to drop it.

Mrs. Choska slapped four dollars on the counter. "All right, all right, here's your money. Just put the melon back."

Bosco laid the melon on the shelf. He grinned as he pocketed the money. "That was a wise decision Mrs. Choska. We'll bring your merchandise to you in a couple of days."

The two men walked toward the door. Usual turned to look at the irate woman. "Nice doing business with you Mrs. Choska."

Boris came from behind the shelves where he had been staying out of sight. He went to his Mother who was still behind the counter. She was crying. He put his arm around his shoulders.

"Don't cry Ma. Those guys won't be around here long. The cops will catch up to them."

Mr. Choska came out of the back room. He was carrying a shotgun. "The next time they pull that stuff, I'm gonna blow their heads off."

Mrs. Choska took the shotgun away from him. "No you're not Choska. We'll go to the police, let them handle it."

Mr. Choska made a dismissive motion with his hands. "Ha, the police, a lot of good that'll do. They're right in there with that no-good Jimmy the Cheese. The guys down at the club were talking about it. We're not the only ones those guys are forcing to buy his lousy bootleg whiskey and scrawny chickens."

Chapter 12

Boris hurried to the clubhouse where Emil, Arnold and Steve were waiting for him.

"Where you been?" Steve asked. "We been waiting for you."

Boris sat at the table. He bent over with his head on his folded arms. The three boys looked at each other.

"What's the matter Boris?" Emil asked.

Boris looked up. He told them what happened in the store. He wiped his eyes. "My Dad said the cops are in with Jimmy the Cheese. They won't do nothing."

"They're all a bunch of crooks," Arnold said.

Emil got up. "The cops aren't in with those crooks. My Uncle Joe is a cop. He told my Dad they just can't get anything on Jimmy the Cheese and his gang. None of the business owners will say anything. They're too scared."

Steve smacked the table. "If the grown ups are too scared to do something about those guys maybe we can."

Arnold nodded. "Yeah, sure. Those crooks got shotguns. What we gonna do . . . throw rocks at them?"

Boris sniffled. He wiped his nose with the back of his hand. "What can we do? We're just four kids who can't even save a little fox from being killed."

"I know, I know," Steve said, "but we can't give up now."

"What can we do about it?" Emil asked.

"I'm working on another plan," Steve said. "But first, we got to get the fox out of the woods before those two crooks shoot it."

Arnold stood. "Maybe we're just wastin our time. None of the traps we set caught him. All we did was catch those two crooks. Now, they think we're part of another gang trying to move in on them."

Emil pointed to Boris. "They got a good look at him. Now they think he's some fat bushy haired crook they call Icepick Pete head of a gang trying to move in on them."

Boris's eyes widened at this. "You think they think I'm that guy?"

"Could be," Steve answered.

Boris let out a long wail. "I'm as good as dead."

Emil pointed at Boris. "Not only that, if they find out he is with us and we're the guys who let their chickens out and Boris caused their still to blow up and, and the barn to burn down, its curtains for us."

"Don't forget we caught those two crooks in our traps too." Arnold added.

Boris bent over the table, his head on his folded arms. "I'm a goner. They'll murderize me," he wailed.

Emil winked. "Yeah Boris, they'll give you a pair of cement overshoes."

"And cement underwear." Emil said, "Then they'll throw you in the river and, and nobody will find you for a hundred years."

Boris began wailing louder than ever. "I'm innocent, I'm innocent. I'll cut off my bushy hair. I'll go on a diet. I'll get skinny like you Arnold."

"Knock it off you guys," Steve said. "First things first. We can't do anything about those crooks but we can save the fox. We need money to buy a good trap that won't hurt the fox."

"And how we getting the money to buy a good trap?" Emil asked.

"We earn it that's how," Steve replied.

"And how do we earn the money?" Arnold asked.

Boris looked up. "We get jobs. We go to work that's how."

"There oughta be some businesses around here that would hire us," Steve said.

Arnold stood up. "Ok, let's go look for jobs. With the four of us working, we can earn enough in no time to buy a couple of traps."

The four boys left the clubhouse.

"Let's go down to the old Muller Rubber Factory," Boris said. "I heard my Dad talking about a new guy in town, a Mr. Bruno, making fireworks in one of the old sheds. Maybe he'll give us jobs. My Dad said he's doing lots of business."

The boys went down past the forlorn looking old building that used to be the Muller Rubber Co. "Spooky looking joint," Arnold said.

"Yeah, I heard it's haunted by a couple of workers who got killed there a long time ago," Emil added.

Boris walked faster past the old factory building. "Boy, you guys sure like to come up with the bad stuff all the time."

Steve pointed to a big shed behind the building. "That's it. That's where they make fireworks."

The boys stopped in front of the shed.

"Where's the sign?" Boris asked.

"Boy what a dummy you are Boris," Arnold said. "Nobody puts up a sign for a fireworks factory. Its against the law to make fireworks."

Steve tried the front door. "It's not locked. Somebody is in there. Let's go in an see if he needs any help."

The four boys went into the office. There was no one there.

Steve looked around. "Anybody here."

There was no answer. Emil walked to the back of the office. He opened the door to the back part of the building. "No one here either."

Emil, Arnold and Steve went into the back area.

"This is where they make the fireworks," Arnold said.

Boris stayed in the outer office. He walked around the room looking at pictures on the wall. A box of cigars was open on the desk. A cigarette lighter shaped like a small pistol was next to the cigars. He took one of the cigars and put it in his mouth. He picked up the lighter and pulled the trigger. Flame shot out the end of the barrel. He put the flame to the end of the cigar and puffed several times. He took a derby hat off a nearby coat rack. He examined it for a moment, then jammed it on his head. He went into the back room where the other boys were walking around looking at the bins of fireworks.

Boris waved the cigar around. "Hey, looka ata me. Im'a Mr. Bruno, the bigga fireworksa man." He strutted toward the other boys waving the derby hat and puffing on the cigar.

The three boys were startled, then scared looks covered their faces. Arnold's face paled. He pointed to the bin of skyrockets beside Boris. He opened his mouth but nothing came out.

Emil turned and ran toward a back door. Steve pointed to the skyrockets. He yelled, "Put that cigar out. This place is one big bomb. You'll blow us up!"

Just then a car drove up next to the building. The boys froze. Boris stood staring at the burning cigar, then, looked around for a place to throw it.

The boys heard voices as two men got out of the car and talked while they walked toward the building.

"It's Jimmy the Cheese and Mr. Bruno," Steve said.

"They'll shoot us," Arnold said as he headed for the back door.

Boris had a terrified look on his face. "Shoot us," he said, then threw the cigar over his shoulder.

It landed in a bin of skyrockets and fireworks. Boris turned and looked at the bin as fuses were lighted and began sizzling.

Steve grabbed Boris's arm. "Come on Boris, run."

Boris was right behind Steve when they got to the door. Jimmy the Cheese and Bruno came in the room just as Boris ran out the back door.

Jimmy the Cheese pointed to the disappearing Boris. "It's him. It's that fat bushy haired guy. It's Icepick Pete."

Bruno nudged Jimmy. He pointed to the sizzling bin of skyrockets and other fireworks. "It's gonna blow." He turned and ran toward the front door.

Jimmy looked around. "Hey Bruno, what, what?" He saw the sizzling bin of fireworks. "It's gonna blow," he yelled and ran toward the front door.

The bin of fireworks and rockets began exploding. Jimmy got to the front door just as the rest of the fireworks began exploding, as the rockets whizzed about the room setting off the other bins.

Jimmy was blown through the front door when the building exploded. Bruno was running down the street yelling, "I quit, I quit."

The four boys were cutting through back yards. Emil, Arnold and Steve had a good lead on Boris who caught up and passed them. They heard the fireworks going off in the building behind them. Within minutes the sound of sirens began splitting the quiet Summer afternoon. The four boys never stopped running or even slowed until they got to their clubhouse. They plopped onto their chairs, breathing hard from their run up the hill away from the fire.

When he was able to breath normally, Steve looked around. "Where's Boris?"

"You mean Boris, the firebug?" Arnold managed to gasp out.

"I heard that," Boris said from under the table. "I ain't no firebug. It was an accident."

Emil looked under the table at him. "Boris, you are a, a Bolshevik."

Boris crawled out from under the table. "What's a Bolshs . . . Bolshi?"

"Crazy guys that go around blowing up buildings, that's what Bolsheviks are," Arnold said.

"Just like you," Emil said.

"It was an accident," Boris wailed as he crawled under the table.

Arnold had a worried look on his face. "You think they saw us before we got out the back door?"

Steve shook his head. "We were outside when they came in but Boris wasn't. They saw him. One of them yelled fat bushy haired guy."

Boris let out another long wail, "I'm a goner. They'll murderize me."

"They think Boris is some guy they keep calling Icepick Pete," Emil said.

"Boy, have we got problems," Steve said. "Those guys think we're another gang trying to move in on them."

"Remember, they saw Boris at the store," Arnold said.

"We got nothing to worry about," Steve said. "You guys heard Bosco say Boris was too dumb looking to be a mobster like that guy Icepick Pete."

Boris poked his head out from under the table. "Oh yeah, I could be a great mobster if I wanted to."

"Sure you could," Emil said. "If Jimmy the Cheese, Bosco and Usual ever find out it's us not another gang and you are the guy they think is Icepick Pete . . ." His voice trailed off as he ran a finger across his throat.

Boris ducked back under the table. He let out another long wail from under the table. "I'm innocent. I didn't mean to do it. They shouldn't leave cigars laying around like that."

Arnold looked under the table. "Remember what we said about cement overshoes?"

Emil looked under the table, "And cement underwear."

Another long wail came from under the table. "I'm innocent. Tell everybody I went to Mexico."

"You guys, cut it out. He's scared enough. If those guys ever figure out Boris really is that fat bushy haired guy giving them all the trouble, they'll connect him to us and its . . ." His voice trailed off.

Arnold finished the sentence, "Curtains for us."

Loud sobs were coming from under the table. "All we wanted to do was save that poor little red fox and help out my May and Pa," Boris said between sobs.

Steve had a thoughtful look on his face. "You guys know what? Sooner or later they'll figure out that fat bushy haired guy really is Boris."

The three boys looked at each other.

"You guys thinking what I'm thinking," Steve said.

Emil and Arnold nodded.

"It's the only way," Arnold said.

"Let's do it," Emil said.

Steve looked under the table at the cowering Boris. "Go in your house, get some scissors."

Boris let a wail louder and longer than the others. "I knew it. I knew it. You guys are gonna kill me. You're gonna stab me with my own scissors to get me out of the way."

"We're not gonna kill you Boris." Steve said. "We'll cut off your bushy hair. Then, we'll all be safe."

Boris came back into the clubhouse. He stood in the door grinning. He wore a cap. The boys looked at him.

"Where's the scissors?" Emil asked.

Boris took off the cap and bowed. "You guys don't need no scissors. His bushy hair was plastered to his head.

Arnold sniffed. He moved away from Boris. "What did you put on your head?"

Chapter 13

The next morning Emil, Arnold and Steve were in the clubhouse waiting for Boris.

"We ain't doing too well at finding jobs," Arnold said.

"That's because Boris blew up the first place we went." Emil said.

Boris came in the clubhouse with a big ice cream cone. Before he could call out the protective words, the boys yelled "Dibs."

A panicked look flashed over his fact that was quickly replaced by a crafty expression. "Sure." he said, then spit all over the ice cream. He handed it toward the others. "Sure, my buddies can have dibs."

"No thanks," they all said together.

He sat at the table. "Then I'll eat it all myself." They watched as Boris gobbled down the ice cream.

"How'd your Mother like your new plastered down hair?" Steve asked.

"We heard her screeching at you all the way back here," Arnold said.

Boris took a big bite out of the ice cream cone. "She said I looked deboner."

"The word is debonair." Steve said.

Steve busied himself writing on a sheet of paper. He considered what he'd written then scratched it off. He wrote some more and stared at it for awhile. He tapped the paper with the pencil. He looked off in the distance while the other boys watched. No one said anything as they waited with expectant looks on their faces.

Finally, Arnold broke the silence. "All right, Ok Mr. President what we doing now?"

"Yeah, you're the smart guy, the boy genius who was taking us to the promised land," Emil said.

"We can't even raise enough money to save that little fox," Arnold said.

Boris joined in. "We might as well give up, forget the fox, forget about Jimmy the Cheese and his gang."

Steve stared at them. He shook his head. "Boy of boy, you guys sure are something else. We have a few problems, you want to quit. You guys talked me into joining this club. I figured the Mound Street Tigers could do some good by helping out Boris's Mom and Dad and, and running those crooks out of town. Now, you guys want to be pussycats instead of tigers, put your tails between your legs and run." He slammed the pencil on the table. "Either this club stands for something besides looking at underwear ads in the magazine, and, and laying around all day or I'm out of it."

The three boys looked at each other. Arnold shrugged. Emil looked away. Boris took another bite out of his ice cream cone. "Looking at underwear ads and laying around all day sounds pretty good to me."

Steve stood. "If that's the way you guys want it, I quit."

Arnold got up. "Shut up Boris. Steve's right. We don't want to be like those hill jacks up on Marcy Street. We got a cause here—really two causes, saving that fox and helping out your Ma and Pa."

Emil studied his folded hands. Boris finished his ice ream cone then leaned back and stared at the ceiling.

Arnold looked up. "All right, so we're tigers instead of pussycats. Let's hear what Steve got to say."

Steve sat down. He picked up the sheet of paper. "We got to find jobs to earn money so we can save the fox first. Then we'll do what we can to harass that Jimmy the Cheese gang so they don't bother honest people anymore."

Chapter 14

Jimmy the Cheese limped down the stairs into the poolroom. Jocko leaned over the counter. He watched as Jimmy lurched to his desk where he sat down groaning as he settled into his chair.

Jocko looked him up and down. "What you been doing, cooking on your grill again?"

Jimmy's hair was scorched, his eyebrows were gone. His shirt was in tatters. One leg of his pants was gone. "You know Jocko, some day your big mouth . . . ."

Jocko held his hands out in a defensive gesture. "No offense Jimmy. I'm just trying to be funny."

Jimmy nodded. "You got the trying right."

Jocko waved a hand toward the outside. "I been hearing sirens for the last half hour." He looked again at Jimmy. "Oh, oh what happened?"

"That crook Icepick Pete blew up my fireworks place. Like to killed me."

"Where's Bruno?"

"He got out before I did. He quit. He's probably halfway to Cleveland by now the way he was running."

"How'd you know it was Icepick who blew up the place?"

"I saw that same bushy haired guy and his gang running out the back door just before the place blew up."

"You got to do something about that guy fast Jimmy before he ruins your business, runs all of us out of town."

Jimmy nodded. "Yeah, Uncle Junie or no Uncle even if that creep is family, something got to be done about him." Jimmy closed his eyes as he leaned back in his chair and groaned. He opened his eyes. "How we doing on cash?"

"Not too good Boss. Nobody's buying anymore of your booze since that goofy Choska was yelling about your lousy stuff making him go blind and paralyzed."

Jimmy groaned. He shook his head. He leaned forward and propped his elbows on his knees. He rested his head on his hands. "Why me? Why me? Why is that dirty rotten crook Icepick picking on me?"

"Hey Boss, that's pretty good, almost like, you know, poetry or something. Icepick picking on me."

Jimmy looked up. He nodded. "Yeah, that's pretty good stuff. Maybe I should go on the radio after I retire from this mobster business if that low down snake in the grass Icepick don't pick me off first."

"There you did it again, Boss," Jocko said.

"Did what?"

"You just came up with another one."

"I did? When?"

"Just now. You don't remember? That fireworks blast musta shook your skull real good. You was talking about a low down crook named Icepick Pete sticking it to you." Jocko laughed. "Hey Boss, How about that? How'd you like that one?"

Jimmy had a glazed look in his eyes along with a puzzled expression on his face.

"Like what one?"

Jocko waved a hand. "Forget it."

Jimmy shook his head. "Now I remember. We was talking about that crooked thief Icepick who spiked my booze Choska was drinking then painted his glasses black so he couldn't see, thought he was blind and paralyzed from drinking my stuffs. Now, nobody's buying nothing."

Jimmy looked around. "Where's Bosco and Usual."

"They left here awhile ago for the farm. Said there's still a lot of chickens out in the woods they got to catch before that chicken stealing fox gets them."

"They better get that fox," Jimmy leaned back in his chair. "I ought'a put a contract out on that chicken stealing fox."

"You've kiddin ain't ya," Jocko said. "That's funny stuff," Jocko said. "A contract on a fox."

Jimmy got up. "I'm heading home. It's been a lousy day."

Jocko watched Jimmy go out the door. He picked up the telephone. He dialed then looked around to see if anyone was listening as the phone range on the other end.

A gruff voice answered, "Yeah."

Jocko looked around again. "This is Jocko. I gotta talk to Uncle Junie."

"Hang on," the voice said.

The man on the other end of the line went to an office. He knocked on the door.

"Yeah, whadda ya want. I'm busy a voice said from the office."

"Telephone for you Junie."

"Who is it?"

"Jocko. He said it's real important. Says he gotta talk to you."

The silver haired man behind the huge polished desk picked up the phone. "What? Make it fast. I'm real busy."

He listened. A bewildered look came over his face. "A contract on a what? A contract on a fox? That goofball Jimmy is putting a contract out on a fox?"

He listened some more. "Keep me posted." He hung up the phone. He covered his face with both hands then slammed them on the desk. Two men dozing in chairs against the far wall on either side of the door were startled awake. They jumped up with guns drawn. "What? What?" they both yelled at the same time waving their guns around.

"Put those guns away you dummies before you shoot each other," Uncle Junie yelled.

The two men put their weapons away, sat down and almost as fast were back dozing again.

Uncle Junie looked at them, shook his head and muttered, "Some bodyguards. The whole German Army could march in here and those guys would be still sleeping."

He stared at the wall. He shook his head. "A contract on a fox—I don't got enough troubles worrying my two moron nephews in Akron don't shoot each other. Now one of them dim bulbs puts out a contract on a fox."

Then, Uncle Junie smiled. He said out loud. "Now if that fox had a gun, I'd hire it to whack both of them dummies."

One of the bodyguards stirred, then sat up, "What, what Boss?"

Junie looked at the man. "I was thinking about putting out a contract on a couple of guys and getting a fox to do the job." He laughed. He slapped the table with both hands. He leaned back in his chair.

"Man, that's funny stuff. I oughta be on the radio telling funny stuff." He laughed again. He glanced at the two bodyguards who were staring at him. He cleared his throat several times then looked down and shuffled papers on his desk, a smile still on his face. The two bodyguards were staring at him with puzzled looks.

"Foxes don't got guns," one of the men said in a low voice not wanting Uncle Junie to hear him.

"Maybe he wants the fox to bite em, do it that way." the other man said.

"Could be."

They looked at each other. Both men shrugged. One man nodded knowingly the said, "That Uncle Junie is one smart guy getting a fox to put a hit on somebody," one of the men said.

The other bodyguard thought for a moment. "Yeah, foxes don't talk they get caught. The cops will never figure out what happened."

Both men gave Uncle Junie admiring looks then dozed off again.

Chapter 15

The four boys were up early the next morning for a meeting in their clubhouse.

Arnold started it off. "Ok we're here. What now?"

Steve looked at the sheet of paper on the table. "We still got to find jobs so we can earn enough money to buy that trap. We better do it soon or those two crooks will get that fox before we can help."

"So where we looking for jobs?" Emil asked.

Boris had a worried look on his face. "Why we gotta work anyway? Why don't we just go steal some junk out of Jake's back fence then sell it back to him like Eddie Beracki does."

Emil smacked him on the shoulder. "You nuts or something? Eddie Beracki got bit by Jake's big dog when he tried to crawl back through that hole in the fence."

"Yeah, right in the butt," Arnold said. You ain't seen how Eddie's walking these days?"

Boris rubbed his butt. "I guess that ain't such a good idea."

Steve listened to the exchange with patience. "We ain't crooks. We don't steal anything. We get jobs, earn money the right way. We start stealing stuff we're just as bad as Jimmy the Cheese and his gang."

Boris stood. He rubbed his butt. "I don't like junk yard dogs anyway."

Steve stood. "Let's go up to Grand Street, see if any of the businesses are hiring."

Before getting to Grand Street, the four boys walked by a house set way back in a bunch of trees. Several cars were parked close to the house. A taxicab pulled into the driveway. Three attractive laughing ladies got out and walked around the back of the house where they rang a bell. The door opened. They went inside. The cab driver backed out of the drive. He stopped before pulling out onto the road, looked out the window at the boys and laughed. "You guys ain't thinking of goin in there are you. It'll cost you a few bucks." He laughed again as he drove out onto the street.

The boys stopped and watched as two more cars drove around behind the house and parked out of sight. One man got out of each car, rang a bell on the side door. It opened. They went inside.

"This looks like a new business," Steve said.

"Maybe they're hiring," Arnold said.

"Let's go see," Emil added.

They passed a sign a short ways down the drive. Boris read the sign, "Happy Times Spa, Cleaning Help Wanted."

Boris danced around jabbing the air a couple of times, "Hey, hey, hee that's a job for me." Before they could stop him Boris was at the back door. He pushed the bell button. The door swung open. Boris went inside.

The door banged open. Boris came stumbling out. A bosomy blond haired woman appeared in the doorway wrapping a negligee around her curvy figure. "And don't come back until you're twenty one," she yelled in a raspy voice.

Boris backed away from the door. A huge man with a shaved head pushed past the woman. He pointed at Boris. "You come back here again I'll break you into little pieces Fatso." He looked over at the other boys. "That goes for youse too you dopey looking bunch of goofs."

Boris put up his fists. "Who you calling Fatso?" He dance around jabbing at the air. "Come out and fight like a man baloney head."

The big man let out a roar as he charged after Boris. For a moment, the surprised Boris stood frozen in a boxer's stance. The big guy was almost on him when Steve yelled, "Run, Boris, run." Emil, Arnold and Steve were already hitting full speed when Steve's shout and the big man's clawing hands almost got to him that Boris was shocked into action. He ducked under the man's huge tattooed arms. Within a few steps he was in full stride with the bellowing big man after him. By the time they all reached the end of the driveway, Boris passed the three boys. The panting, yelling big man gained on the three boys. They split up and each went in a different direction. The big man pulled up looking from one disappearing boy to the next as they melted into the surrounding shrubs and bushes as they ran through back yards leaving the big man behind. He stood shaking his fist and yelling at them.

The three boys made it back to Mound Street. Boris was nowhere in sight. They stopped to catch their breath. Emil was bent over holding his side. "Boris will get all of us killed someday when he mouths off like that."

"We gotta talk to him, shut him up or we're all dead," Arnold gasped taking deep breaths. Steve sat on the curb. When he was able to catch his breath and talk, he said, "That's it. Boris got to keep his mouth shut or we suspend him from the club for awhile." "Ha," Arnold said breathing easier now. "That's like asking Reverend Shushnic to stop praying."

The three boys walked back to the clubhouse. Boris was sitting at the table eating a candy bar with one hand while petting the stiff dried out dead cat with his other one. He looked at the three boys as they came in. "What's up?" He sprayed candy bits as he said it. The three boys glanced at each other, Emil lunged across the table at Boris. Steve and Arnold caught him before he could get his hands on Boris's neck.

Emil struggled to get loose. "Let me at him. I'll kill him before he kills us."

Arnold and Steve pushed him into a chair. "Sit down and shut up," Steve said. "We'll hold court and decide what to do with him."

Steve moved over until he was opposite Boris. He picked up a rock and pounded the table several times. "The court of the Mound Street Tigers will now come to order in the case of Boris Choska whose big mouth and goofy actions almost got us killed again. We have several causes of action against him." He picked up a sheet of paper. Boris stared at the table while Steve read the charges.

"Action number one: He caused some crook's barn and whiskey still to blow up. Action two, he blew up a fireworks factory. Action three, he lipped off to a big guy who said he would break us into little pieces he saw us again."

He pounded the rock on the table twice. He pointed at Boris, the defendant slouching in his chair staring at the floor with a defiant look on his face.

"What say you Boris Choska to these charges?"

Boris looked up. "This court ain't legal. I don't got no lawyer. I don't got no money for a lawyer so this court got to get one for me and pay for it. That's the law." The three boys stared at Boris.

"He's right," Steve said. "We can't hold a trial less he has a lawyer. We don't have any money to hire one, so, we'll have to let the defendant off."

He banged the rock on the table. "All causes of action and charges against Boris Choska are hereby dismissed because the nutty guy can't afford a lawyer."

Boris leaped to his feet. He shook his fist in the air. "I resemble that remark your honor. I'm not nutty, just too smart for you guys. You'll never be able to pin anything on Boris the Great. I'm too slick, too smart, too brave for you guys". He raised a fist in the air. "Boris the Great marches on." He marched toward the door, head up, shoulders back, then tripped over his own feet and fell. He got up. He yelled, "Charge," and ran through the door. He came running back inside, yelling, "Here they come, then dove under the table. "Tell em I went to Africa. Tell em I joined the Marines."

Bosco kicked the door open. He and Usual walked in. Bosco looked over the three startled boys.

"They are just as goofy looking as the first time we saw em," he said.

Usual pushed his straw hat to the back of his head. He pulled a dirty handkerchief out of his back pocket and wiped his sweating brow. "I told you we're wasting our time coming here. These guys look too dumb to be tied in with a crook as stupid as Icepick."

Bosco shook his head. "I dunno Usual. These guys could be the perfect front for a crook trying to muscle in on us."

He looked at each boy then counted, "One, two, three, there's only three of them. Every time we saw them before, there was four. One's missing."

"You're a genius Bosco for figuring that out. If there's four and one's missing that leaves three," Usual said.

Bosco put a hand on Usual's neck and squeezed, "If there wasn't three witnesses here I'd crack your neck you fat little tomato head."

"I was just kidding Bosco. You're right, there was four of em. That fat kid with the bushy hair, just like Icepick was disguising himself ain't here."

Bosco took his hand off Usual's neck. He glared at Steve. "Ok, four eyes, where's the fat kid with the bushy hair."

Steve gave him the hands palms up how do I know gesture. Boris sneezed. Steve kicked Boris under the table.

"What was that?" Bosco asked.

Usual pointed to the table. "It came from under there." He bent over to look under the table. He straightened up.

"Who's under there sneezing?" Bosco asked.

"I don't see nobody, just a big box."

Steve reached under the table. He felt around in the box. He grabbed the stiff dried out dead cat by the tail. He held it up. "It was him that sneezed. Our pet cat Arthur."

Bosco and Usual stepped back from the 6table.

"Geez, a cat," Usual said.

"A cat that sneezes," Bosco said leaning over the table to get a closer look at Arthur.

Bosco poked the cat with his finger. "Hey, this cat's deader'n a doornail."

"If it's dead, how can it sneeze?" Usual asked.

Bosco glared at Steve. "Hey, what you guys trying to pull? This cats dead. It's dried out and stiff as a board. How can a dead cat sneeze?"

Steve never missed a beat. He looked at Bosco. "Sir, that's what we been trying to figure out ever since we got Arthur."

Usual was already at the clubhouse door. He turned motioning to Bosco. "Let's get out of here. This place gives me the creeps with these goofy looking kids claiming they got a dead cat that sneezes. I told you they was nuts. Besides, you were right the first time, they even look too dumb to be tied in with a crook like Icepick Pete."

Bosco followed Usual to the door. "Let's get away from these nutty kids, go in the nice quiet woods, get that fox before Jimmy comes out starts counting his chickens again," he said.

As they went out the door Usual asked, "Why is Jimmy so hung up on raising chickens when he can make so much money making and selling booze?"

Bosco shrugged. "I dunno. I asked him once. He told me he grew up on a farm. He's got a thing about raising chickens. He used to talk about it all the time we was in jail. He said he wanted to retire from being a crook someday, raise chickens."

"That Jimmy the Cheese may be a tough guy but he sure got a soft spot for chickens," Usual said as they walked away from the clubhouse.

Arnold went to the door. "They're gone. You can come out now Boris."

Steve let the dead cat fall to the floor. "Aargh, I never thought I'd pick up a lousy dead cat."

Boris came out from under the table. "What you doing calling Arthur lousy? He just saved my life and maybe you guy's lives too."

"Yeah sure," Emil said. "The cat saved your life for now if you don't do no more dumb things and quit mouthing off."

Arnold jabbed a finger toward Boris. "All we got to worry about now is the word getting around that we got a dead cat in here that sneezes and that we're nutty as a bunch of squirrels."

"So be it," Steve said, "but we still got the problem of saving that fox from those guys."

Chapter 16

The next morning Steve, Emil and Arnold went to Choska's store. They sat on the big yellow milk bottle storage boxes waiting for Boris to come out. They heard Mrs. Choska inside the store yelling at Mr. Choska and Boris calling them lazy loafers and she had to do everything around the store. The side door opened. Boris slipped out taking a last look inside to see of his Mother saw him leaving. He sat on one of the boxes and leaned against the wall. "What we doing today?"

Emil slid off the box. "I don't know what we're doing today but I know what I'm doing right now. I'm leaving." He pointed down the street. "Here comes Eddie Beracki."

"Too late," Steve said. "He's spotted us."

Eddie Beracki, a big kid, walked with a slouch that made him look like an old man shuffling into a stiff head wind, saw the four boys and walked faster toward them. He was about seventeen or eighteen as far as anyone in the neighborhood knew. He was a funny looking kid with his long red hair slicked back with cheap hair tonic that could be smelled from ten feet away. He had a white puffy face topped by one red eyebrow that stretched across his forehead and close set pale blue eyes that unnerved even adults when he stared at them.

Eddie claimed he was a businessmans. His main business was selling protection to other kids in the neighborhood. The protection he sold was that he wouldn't beat them up if they paid him a nickel a week. Eddie left school by mutual agreement between him, teachers and the Principal after spending two years in the fourth grade and heading toward a third one with no prospects for ever leaving the fourth grade. Eddie always said that school was for dumb guys who didn't know nothing and had to learn stuff there.

Eddie shuffled up to where the boys sat on the big yellow milk bottle storage boxes. Boris panicked. "My Ma's calling me." He jumped off the box and headed toward the stores side door. Eddie grabbed him by the shirt before he got two steps away. "Not so fast Fatso." He pulled Boris away from the door. "Sit down. I got a deal for you guys. You can make a lot of money throwing in with Eddie Beracki in my new business."

Emil slid off his box. "I ain't stealing no junk from Jake's junkyard if that's your new business."

Eddie grabbed Emil by his shirt front. He pulled the smaller boy right up on his tip toes. "You gonna listen or do I pound on your head for awhile till you do?"

"Yeah, Eddie, I'll listen," Emil was able to gurgle. Eddie let the smaller boy go. He looked at Steve and Arnold. "You guys wanna hear what I got to say or do I bust your heads you listen anyway?"

Arnold nodded. "Yeah, yeah, we'll listen. Won't we Steve."

Steve looked at Eddie's scrunched up face then at his doubled up fists. He decided real quick it was in his and the other boys best interests to listen to Eddie's latest money making deal. Eddie dug into the pocket of the brown double breasted pin stripe suit coat he wore every day Winter and Summer. It had seen better days and was cleaned a few years before the Salvation Army threw it out and Eddie rescued it. He pulled out a golf ball. He held it up. "Here it is. This is your ticket to thousands, maybe even millions."

Boris leaned over and examined it up close. "Looks like a golf ball to me."

Eddie banged the ball on Boris's head.

"Ow," Boris yelled. "That smarts."

Eddie held the ball over Boris's head. "You wanta listen or do I gotta bang you on the head some more?"

Boris covered his head with both hands. "I'll listen Mr. Eddie, honest, I'll listen."

Eddie looked at the other boys. "You guys gonna listen or do I gotta bang all your heads so's you can make thousands, even millions?"

Steve made a slight nodding motion with his head. "We'll listen Mr. Beracki, we'll listen. We have to make some money to save a fox."

Eddie shook his head. "Shush, you guys want to make money to save a fox and everybody thinks I'm nuts."

He reached into his pocket and took out a bunch of golf balls. He held them out. "Ain't they pretty? I get em outta the water at the golf course. You guys know Eddie Beracki is King of the Swampers."

He looked around, then moved closer to the boys. He lowered his voice. "I invented a secret way to make these old golf balls look like new. I sell em to the stiffs at the golf course who think I stole em. Those office guys buy anything they think you stole it."

Eddie looked around again like he was passing on some big military secret. "I want you guys to be my salesmens for my fine like new golf balls. You'll make a ton of money selling em. They'll go like, like . . . ."

"Hotcakes," Steve said. "They'll go like hotcakes."

"Yeah, yeah, like hotcakes. You guys come with me. I'll show you my factory and my secret way to make them balls look like new."

The four boys looked at each other. Steve shrugged. "Why not? We have to make money so we can buy that fox trap."

Eddie motioned for the boys to follow as he shuffled down Mound Street. He kept shaking his head as he walked. "Gotta make money to save a fox," he kept muttering.

Eddie took the four boys behind a dilapidated house at the far end of Mound Street where it trailed off into a woods. He had them sit at a makeshift table while he went into a propped up old shed and brought out a bucket of golf balls and a pail of water.

"Before I show you guys my secret invention, I'm telling you right now, I bust your heads you tell anyone how I do it."

Boris raised his right hand. "We won't tell anyone, honest Mr. Eddie. Right you guys?" The other boys nodded.

"We just want to make some money Mr. Beracki," Steve said.

"Yeah, to save some fox," Eddie said. He looked real hard and long at each one of the boys. He raised his fist. "This is what you get you tell my secret."

Eddie began the demonstration of his new invention. He dipped a ball with several gashes into the pail of water. "First, you wash the ball real good. Then you dries it with a clean rag." He reached into a box under the table. He held up a bar of Ivory soap. He scraped off several slivers of soap and filled in the gashes in the ball. He took a pencil stub out of his shirt pocket and made indentations in the soap to match the other ones on the ball. He then took a bottle of white shoe polish out of the box under the table. He held it up for the boys to see. He tapped the bottle. "This here is my secret stuffs that makes them balls look like new."

He spread the white shoe polish over the ball. He let it dry for awhile then opened a small can of red paint. With a small brush he put a red dot on the ball. He held the ball up for the boys to see . . . "Just like a new Spalding Red Dot."

He took a bar of clear wax out of the box and sliced off several pieces. He rubbed the wax over the ball then held it up for the boys to see. "Look at that. Just like new."

The boys glanced at Steve who shrugged. Eddie saw the looks they gave each other. He grabbed Emil who sat nearest to him in a headlock. "I saw that. You guys try to back out now after I showed you my secret invention, I'll squeeze all your heads till they pop like watermelons." He gave the gasping Emil's head a squeeze then let him go. "You guys with me so you can make lots of money to save your fox or . . ." He made a move toward Boris who jumped out of his way. "I'm with you all the way, Mr. Eddie."

Eddie glared at Steve and Arnold who nodded as they left the table and backed away. "We'll do it Mr. Beracki," Steve said as he looked at Arnold who appeared to be saying yes but nothing came out of his mouth.

Eddie stared at each boy with those little close set eyes of his. "Ok, then you guys be at the golf course tomorrow at 8 o'clock. I'll show youse guys how to make lots of money selling Eddie's fine like new golf balls."

Chapter 17

The four boys met at the clubhouse and rode their bicycles out to the golf course. They hid their bicycles in the underbrush across the road from the golf course then walked over to the parking lot to wait for Eddie. They saw him riding toward the clubhouse with two bags hanging from his handlebars. He took his bicycle into the bushes then came out carrying the two bags of golf balls. He motioned for the four boys to follow him into the parking lot.

"Here's where you sell these guys when they get out of their cars before they go in the clubhouse. You got to act kinda secret like so they think you stole the balls. Like I told you, these office stiffs will buy anything if they think you stole it."

Within a few minutes, a car drove into the parking lot. Four big heavyset men got out. They went to the trunk to get out their golf clubs.

Eddie picked up a bag of his golf balls. "You guys watch how I do it."

He walked over to the four men. The boys saw him open the bag and show the four men his like new balls. They couldn't get in to their pockets fast enough to buy the whole bag.

Eddie went to where the four boys were watching. "Two bucks. I sold the whole for two bucks. It's like picking cherries."

He held up the other bag of balls. "We're all gonna get rich selling Eddie's fine like new golf balls. I'm goin over to those other guys waitin to play. You guys watch. I'll sell this whole bag in a couple of minutes."

When Eddie was on his way to the first tee, Steve said, "Boy, this is gonna be fun when those guys hit Eddie's fine like new golf balls. Let's go watch."

The four boys stayed behind a car in the parking lot near the first tee when the four big golfers were practicing their swings and loosening up. The biggest one of the four stuck a tee in the ground. He took out of his pocket one of Eddie's like new balls and put it on the tee. He got in position to hit his drive. His four friends watched as the big man wiggled a few times as he placed the club head by the ball. After a few seconds of concentration, he took his driver back real slow, then came down at the ball in a ferocious swing.

When the club head hit the ball, pieces flew in all directions.

"You busted the ball," one of the other golfers said.

"Wow, what a swing," another one added.

"Oh yeah, watch this one," the big guy said as he teed up another one of Eddie's fine like new golf balls. He let go with another mighty swing. The ball exploded into flying pieces of soap. One of his buddies picked up a piece from the hall. He rubbed it between two fingers. "Hey, you been smacking soap balls."

The big golfer picked up a piece. He rubbed it between his fingers the smelled it. He took a couple more out of his pocket. He ran his fingernail over the covers digging soap out of the cuts. Just then, Eddie came up to another foursome waiting to tee off. He didn't see what happened with the two balls the big man hit. He went up to the waiting foursome. "Hey,' he said looking around like he didn't want anybody seeing him selling hot stuff. "You guys wanna buy some like new golf balls real cheap?"

The four big golfers on the tee who were scratching soap out of their golf balls turned around at the sound of Eddie's voice.

"You," the big man who hit the soap balls yelled at Eddie.

"Get him," a second man shouted as he started after Eddie.

The four men grabbed Eddie. They turned him upside down, held him up by his ankles and bounced his head off the ground. Golf balls and coins fell out of Eddie's pockets as he yelled, "I sell only good stuffs. I got a money back guarantee."

Steve gestured to the other three boys. "Time to go."

The boys got their bicycles and rode back to their clubhouse.

"What we tryin next?" Emil asked.

"We'll try caddying," Steve answered. "I saw those guys getting paid a dollar for carrying golfers' clubs around. We'll go out to the golf course tomorrow. With the four of us making a dollar apiece, we'll have enough money to buy that trap pretty quick."

Chapter 18

The next morning the four boys met at the clubhouse. They walked to the corner of Crow and Main Street where they planned to hitchhike out to the golf course.

"Boris, you hitchhike first," Steve said.

"Why me? Why do I gotta stand out in the hot sun while you guys are in the shade?"

Emil was already sitting with his back against a tree. "Because we said so."

Arnold sat next to Emil. "That's what you get for almost getting us killed by lipping off to those crooks."

Boris went out and stood by the curb. "It ain't fair," he said.

"Oh shut up Boris and quit whining." Steve said. When you see a car coming put out your thumb. A driver will stop for one guy. When he does, the rest of us will pile in the car too."

Several cars went by. The drivers took one look at Boris and sped by.

Boris stepped back in the shade of the tree. "It's too hot out there."

Steve saw a car coming. "Here comes one. Get out there Boris."

Boris went back to the curb and stuck out his thumb. The driver slowed when he saw Boris then stopped. The bald headed driver leaned over and opened the passenger side door. He gave Boris a smile showing yellow horse like false teeth. "Hi big guy. You wanna ride? Hop in." His voice was high and silky smooth.

Boris was at the car door ready to get in. "Gee thanks Mister. I got some buddies want to go too."

Steve, Emil and Arnold hurried to the car. The driver took one look. He pointed to his back seat filled with boxes. "Sorry fellas, I can only take one."

Boris started to get in the car. "That's Ok Mister, I'll go."

Emil and Arnold each grabbed one of Boris's arms and pulled him back. "Sorry, Mister, his Mother told us to stick together."

The driver pulled the door closed then said through the open window, "Maybe next time big fella," then drove off screeching his tires.

Boris jerked his arms free from Emil and Arnold. "What you guys do that for? I'm hot and tired standing out there. I could a had a ride to the golf course."

"You know who that was," Emil asked.

Boris shook his head.

"That was Colonial Mac," Arnold said.

"Who's he?"

Emil shook his head. "Boy Boris, you don't know nothing."

"He's one of those funny guys," Arnold said.

Boris had a puzzled look on his face. "What's a funny guy?"

Arnold jerked a thumb toward Steve. "A funny guy is like, like Emil's Uncle Freddie."

"Yeah," Emil said. "My Ma tells me to stay away from him."

Boris was still puzzled. "Why do you guys call him a funny guy?"

Arnold shrugged. "Maybe because funny guys do funny things."

"What kind of funny things?"

Emil and Arnold looked at each other. They each shrugged their shoulders, then, Emil said, "I heard that funny guys go around biting people in the butt."

"See Boris, we saved you from getting bit in the butt by Colonial Mac," Steve said.

Boris rubbed his butt with both hands as the boys walked down Main Street.

Chapter 19

Back at Jimmy's poolroom, Bosco and Usual sat waiting for Jimmy the Cheese to come out of his office. They had glum expressions on their faces. Both men were dressed in golfers clothes—green pants, yellow shirts and long billed golfers' caps. Jocko came down the stairs into the poolroom. He stopped short when he saw the two men sitting with grim looks on their faces.

"What're you guys doin? Why you dressed in those costumes? It ain't Halloween yet."

He laughed as he pointed to their clothes but stopped when Bosco got up from his chair and started after him. Jocko went behind the counter in a hurry. "Now, now Bosco, I'm just kiddin."

Usual grabbed Bosco's arm and held him back. "Leave him alone Bosco. He's a goof who thinks he's funny."

Bosco tried to pull away. "I'll make him funny looking when I get through with him."

Jimmy the Cheese came out of his office. He was dressed in checkered knickers, red sox, a green shirt and a red tam with a tassel on top.

Jocko stared at Jimmy. "Geez, what is this? You guys goin to some kind of masquerade party or something?"

Jimmy made a motion like a practice golf swing. "We're gonna play golf today. Lots of businessmens play golf. We're businessmens so we got to get in with the businessmens in the neighborhood."

He motioned for Bosco and Usual to follow as he went out the door. "Be back in a couple of hours," he said.

Jocko leaned over the counter and watched the three men go out the door. He shook his head. "I wouldn't have believed it unless I saw it."

The four boys got to the course early before play started. They walked down to the caddie shack where caddies sat on the ground waiting for the shack to open when the caddy master would pick out caddies for the foursomes that were starting to arrive.

Steve, Emil, Arnold and Boris looked around at the other boys who were watching them.

"Don't look now," Steve said. "Those big guys over there are sizing us up."

So Boris looked over at the four big guys watching them.

Emil elbowed Boris. "He said don't look so what did you do, you looked."

One of the big kids, the biggest meanest looking one, got up. He walked toward the boys.

Steve made a slight motion with his head. "Don't look. Here comes one of them."

So Boris looked again.

"You guys keep quiet," Steve said. "I'll handle this.'

The big mean looking kid walked to where the four boys sat. He towered over them. He glared at each one of them in turn. "You guys ain't never caddied here before, right?"

Boris looked up at him. "No sir. This our first time. We came out here to make some . . ." he cut off when Arnold jabbed him in the ribs. "Shut up Boris."

Steve got up. "Yes sir. We would like to get jobs caddying."

The big kid gave Steve a lopsided grin. "Oh you guys would like to caddy here would ya?"

Steve nodded. The big kid moved closer to Steve who came up to his chest. Steve looked up at him.

The big mean looking kid looked down at Steve. His lopsided mean grin became more lopsided and meaner.

"You guys can't caddy here less you been cricked."

Boris had a scared look on his face. "What's cricked?"

The big kid looked down at Boris. "The fat guy sure talks a lot."

Boris started to get up. He got out "I ain't . . ." but Emil pulled him back down.

"Sit down and shut up Boris," he said.

The big kid pointed toward the stream flowing behind the caddy shack. "You guys see that crick? We throw you in, you been cricked. Then you can caddy here. You don't wanna get cricked, you get cricked anyway then we beat you up. Maybe, if you can still walk, you can caddy here."

Boris got up. He ran to the stream and jumped in. The big mean looking kid laughed. "That fat guy, he can run like a scared rabbit. Maybe he is a scared rabbit."

Steve moved closer to the big kid. He looked up at him. He pointed at the kid's chest. "Sir, under Article Twelve of the United States Constitution, you are violating our right to seek gainful employment."

"Issat so. How do you figure that Shorty?"

"By forcibly throwing us in a body of water you are," Steve ticked off on his fingers the points he was making. "One, threatening us in a violent manner in order for us to work which is a crime according to the Criminal Laws of the United States Government. Two, it is a serious violation of the United States Labor Laws and three, such actions by you could result in serious punishment, like twenty years in jail with only bread and water to eat if the rats as big as cats don't get it first and if the cockroaches and spiders haven't eaten you alive already."

The big mean looking kid stared down at Steve. He started to say something but nothing came out. Steve knew he now had the kid on the ropes. He pressed his attack. "If you don't beat us up or throw us in the creek I won't make a citizens arrest on you and your friends."

The big kid stepped back from Steve. "You talking about arresting us?"

"Yessir. Under the authority of the Bill of Rights and the Constitution of the United States Article Fifteen, a citizen of said United States can affect a citizens arrest when he observes a felony being committed. By denying us the right to work without being assaulted first, you and your friends are committing a felony. So, I have the authority vested in me by the Constitution of the United States to make a citizens arrest."

By now, the big mean looking kid looked concerned. "You some kind of Fed sent here to spy on us?"

"You might say that. You can check with your Union to see if what I'm saying is right."

The big kid scratched his head. "Union, We ain't got no Union."

Steve gave him a surprised look. "You don't have a Union?"

"Then maybe I can go easy on you."

"Gee thanks Shorty." He put his arm around Steve's shoulder. "You're OK Shorty."

"You guys ought to have a Union."

"We should?"

"What kind of benefits you guys got like sick pay, vacations and vacation pay?"

The big kid scratched his head again. He looked bewildered. "We ain't got no sick pay, no vacation pay. We ain't even got vacations. We got to work all the time."

"Out in the hot sun?"

"Yeah, out in the hot sun."

"You guys need a Union. That way, you can get higher pay, vacations, vacation pay, all the things other guys get in Unions. If they don't give it to you, you guys go on strike. You don't work until the company agrees to give it to you. You shut the place down. Nobody gets to play golf until they give you what you want."

The big mean looking kid patted Steve's shoulder. "You're Ok Shorty. Come on over here and tell the other guys how we should get us a Union."

Steve backed away from the big kid. "I charge a dollar for giving Union advice."

The big kid grabbed Steve by the arm. "Ok, you got a deal Shorty. Come on over here and tell the other guys about a Union."

Steve looked at the other boys, shrugged, then went with the big kid. The boys watched as the other caddies gathered around while Steve told them about forming a Union and going on strike if they didn't get more pay and vacations. Within a few minutes, the caddies were milling around in front of the Caddy shack when it opened and the Caddymaster began calling for caddies. He pointed at the big kid and three other boys.

"Ok Stash, you, you and you got the first loop." He pointed up to the first tee where four golfers were practicing their swings. "You guys got that foursome up on the first tee."

The four boys didn't move. The Caddymaster looked at them. "What, what? Get over there. Those guys are ready to go."

The four boys just stood there.

The Caddymaster pointed again at the golfers on the tee. "Get up there now," he yelled.

"We ain't goin," Stash said.

"Whadda you mean you ain't goin?"

"That's just what I said. We ain't goin."

The Caddymaster jabbed a finger at the four caddies. "You guys are fired."

Stash laughed. "You can't fire us. We're on strike."

The Caddymaster leaned over the counter. "You're on what? Are you guys nuts or something?"

He motioned to the other boys sitting on the grass just beyond the caddyshack. "You four guys, get up to the first tee. They're waiting for you."

The four boys didn't move. The Caddymaster yelled. "What's the matter with you guys? You all gone crazy?"

"We're on strike," the four boys yelled back at him.

The Caddymaster had a panicked look on his face. "We got a full schedule of golfing today. We need caddies."

"We want more money." Stash said.

"We want paid vacations," another caddy yelled from the crowd.

"We want better working conditions," another boy yelled.

"We want benefits." another shouted, then turned to the kid sitting next to him and asked, "What's benefits?"

The other boy shrugged. "I dunno but that little guy with the glasses said we should have em."

The Caddymaster gripped the counter. "You guys are all crazy. Who started all this stuff about a Union, about a strike?"

Stash pointed to Steve who was back sitting with Emil, Arnold and Boris.

"That little guy with the glasses did. He knows all about Unions and stuff. He told us we should have a Union and go on strike to get more money and, and benefits and vacations and stuff like that. We ain't caddying till we get what we want."

Caddymaster looked over to where Steve sat with the three other Mount Street Tigers. He pointed to them. "Communists, you guys are Communists . . . that's what you guys are. I'm calling the cops. I'm calling the FBI. You Commies are going to jail."

The caddies, with Stash leading began walking around in front of the caddy shack yelling, "We want more money. We want vacations."

The phone rang in the caddy shack. The Caddymaster snatched it up. He listened for a moment then yelled into it, "I ain't got no caddies. They're all on strike. Some midget Communist came in here, got em all worked up about getting more money and paid vacations and stuff like that. They're marching around here with Communist signs yelling they got a Union, they're on strike. Communists, they're all over the place."

The phone rang again and again. Each time the Caddymaster picked it up and yelled into it. "I ain't go no caddies. They're all on strike. They say they got a Union and won't caddy till they get more money and benefits. Some Communist, a little guy with a gun came in here with a gang, they all got guns and waving red flags, got the caddies all riled up. I'm telling you they won't work. Tell the golfers they got to carry their own bags. I'm calling the cops and the FBI."

Chapter 20

Jimmy the Cheese's battered old black Cadillac drove into the golf course parking lot. Eddie was hiding in the bushes watching as Jimmy, Bosco and Usual got out of the car. Usual and Bosco took the golf bags out of the trunk.

"Hey Bosco, get us some caddies, you know the guys what carry our clubs," Jimmy said as he took a practice swing without a club.

"Looking good Boss," Usual said.

"I know," Jimmy said as he took a few more awkward practice swings.

Eddie hurried out of his hiding place. He caught up with Bosco. He showed the big man his like new golf balls. Bosco looked at the balls then at Eddie. He couldn't get the money out of his pocket fast enough to buy the whole bag. Eddie hurried back into the bushes, got on his bicycle and headed back to the neighborhood as fast as he could go.

Bosco watched Eddie ride away. "The guy's a real crook stealing golf balls," thought Bosco as he went on toward the caddy shack.

Jimmy the Cheese and Usual were on the first tee waiting for Bosco. Jimmy looked at his watch.

"What's keeping Bosco? We got a. a . . . ?"

"Tee time, we got a tee time," Usual said.

"That's what I just said."

Jimmy held his hands out palms up. "Where's the caddies?" Jimmy asked when Bosco came back.

"There ain't none," Bosco said. "They're on strike. They got a Union."

"Whadda ya mean there ain't none, they're on strike?"

"Some little guy, a Communist came in here waving a gun with a gang, all, of em carrying guns and red Commie flags, got all the kids riled up about more money and stuff so they made up a Union, went on strike. They guy they call the Caddymaster said they had a crazy man with em, runnin around yellin, even jumped in the crick, a fat . . ." Bosco looked at Jimmy the Cheese and Usual. They all said at the same time, "bushy haired guy."

Jimmy shook his head. "Now that crook Icepick Pete is in the Union racket. Why didn't I think of that?"

"But, but Boss, this running around yelling crazy fat man don't got bushy hair," Usual said.

Jimmy waved a hand. "Wasn't wearing that bushy haired wig. A master of disguise, that Icepick."

Usual glanced at Bosco and shrugged.

Bosco held out the bag of balls he just bought from Eddie Beracki. He took one out of the bag and showed it to Jimmy and Usual. "Like new balls. I gave the kid a buck for the bag. He grabbed the buck, ran back in the woods. He musta stole em."

Jimmy looked at the ball. "Looks like you made a good deal Bosco."

He motioned to Bosco and Usual. "You guys get the bags. We don't need none of that crook Icepick's lousy Commie Union caddies anyway. You guys carry my bag."

The other golfers had teed off and were way down the fairway when Jimmy, Usual and Bosco got there.

"You go first Boss," Usual said.

Jimmy teed up the like new ball Bosco gave him. He stood off to the side with his driver taking practice swings.

"Lookin good Boss," Bosco said.

"Yeah, you're lookin real good Boss," Usual said.

Jimmy grunted. He stepped up to the ball, wiggled his butt a few times, then took a slow backswing and came down hard on the ball. When the club head hit the ball, pieces of soap flew in every direction.

"Bomb," Jimmy yelled. He dropped his club. He started to run one way, then another. He kept yelling, "bomb, bomb" as he ran to a nearby pond and jumped in.

"Bomb, bomb," Bosco yelled as he ran after Jimmy and dove into the pond.

Usual started toward the clubhouse yelling, "bomb, bomb," then reversed course and followed Jimmy and Bosco into the pond.

Everything was quite for awhile. The only sounds heard was the chanting of the caddies down by the caddy shack. Jimmy came up out of the water real slow. Seaweed was draped across his head. Bosco and Usual came up sputtering and coughing water.

The three men sloshed out of the water. Usual went to the tee. He picked up pieces of soap that came out of the ball Jimmy hit. He rubbed the piece of soap between his fingers. He sniffed it.

He handed the piece to Jimmy saying, "You hit a ball with soap in it."

Jimmy rubbed the piece of soap between his fingers then sniffed it. He looked at Bosco. "That kid stiffed you. He's one of Icepick's gang. He wanted us to think those soap balls was bombs just to scare me."

"But, but I got a good deal Boss."

Chapter 21

A wet and not happy Jimmy the Cheese went into the poolroom followed by a still dripping Bosco and Usual we were pulling seaweed out of their hair and off their clothes. Jocko looked up from his calculator. The unlit cigar dropped from his mouth as his jaw opened in surprise.

"I thought youse guys was going to play golf, not go swimming."

Jimmy growled and grunted a reply then went into his office without even looking at Jocko. Bosco glared at Jocko then reached across the counter. He made a grab for Jocko who had vacated his chair and was backing away from Bosco fast as he could. "That's it Jocko, that's it. I'm tearing your head off right now."

He started to climb over the counter. Usual grabbed him from behind. "Leggo," Bosco yelled. "I'll break his scrawny neck."

Jimmy came out of the back office. "What's going on out here?"

"Bosco's trying to kill me," Jocko yelled as he went past Jimmy into the back office, slammed and locked the door. Jimmy helped Usual pull Bosco off the counter. "Calm down Bosco. This ain't no time to fight between ourselves. We got bigger problems with that Icepick out there harassing us, trying to move into my business now he's in the Union racket. We gotta have a meeting now. This is getting out of hand."

Bosco and Usual followed Jimmy back into the office. Jocko scurried out of the glaring Bosco's way. Usual closed the office door. Jimmy had changed into dry clothes. He sat at his desk. He lit a big cigar and began puffing hard as he regarded Bosco.

"Ok, ok, who sold you those soap balls. The guy knew we'd think they was bombs or something trying to scare me."

Bosco shifted uneasily in his seat. "Some big kid, goofy looking with slicked down red hair, wearing a brown suit coat, funny looking face, staring eyes that gave me the creeps."

Jimmy took the cigar out of his mouth. "One of Icepick's goons. He's got a bigger gang than we thought. What about this Union and strike stuff with them caddies?"

Bosco thought for a moment. He clenched his fists. "It was a little guy wearing them thick glasses. A Communist the Caddymaster called him. Said he was a Communist came in to agitate the caddies, get them to start a Union and, and go on strike. That's why we couldn't get no caddies. They was all on strike."

Jimmy stared at the ceiling while he puffed on his cigar. He looked at Bosco and Usual.

"Icepick again. That little guy was no Communist. He was one of Icepick's gang. That no good crook ain't satisfied trying to take over my booze and fireworks business, he got to blow em up. Now, he's into the Union rackets. It just ain't patriotic. We got a war on and the greedy crook is, is . . . just plain un-American starting a strike, hurting the war effort."

Bosco pointed a finger at Jimmy. "We gotta stop fooling around with this guy. It's time we break his legs. The sooner the better."

Usual nodded. "Yeah, Jimmy, we got to get this guy Icepick once and for all."

Jimmy shook his head. "That's the old way of doing things. We beat up Icepick, we got trouble with the cops, we got trouble with Uncle Junie. He don't want nothing to happen to Icepick. I done told you guys that no good crook Icepick is his nephew. We got to put our smarts to work, figure out another way to run that lousy creep out of town."

"How we doin that?" Usual asked.

"Yeah, we been playing fair while he's been trying to whack us," Bosco said.

Jimmy took the cigar out of his mouth. He leaned over his desk. He looked around to make sure no one else was listening to what he was about to say. He tapped his forefinger on the desk.

"I'm working on a plan to take care of that guy once and for all."

"What kind of plan Boss?" Usual said.

Bosco and Usual leaned closer to the desk to hear Jimmy give his plan. Jimmy leaned back in his chair. He locked his fingers behind his head. He took a couple more puffs on his cigar. He lunged forward. He pointed at both Usual and Bosco. The two men had expectant looks on their faces. "I don't got it done yet. I'm still working on it."

Chapter 22

Emil and Arnold went into the Mound Street Tigers clubhouse. Steve was sitting at his usual spot at the table. Arnold looked around. "Where's Boris? He hiding under the table again?"

Steve shrugged. "Haven't seen him yet."

Emil looked at Steve who was writing on a sheet of paper in front of him. "What now Mr. Genius?"

"I'm thinking, I'm thinking," Steve said as he went on writing.

Emil shook his head. "Maybe we ought to give up on saving that fox."

Arnold nodded. "Yeah, maybe Emil's right. Everything we tried so far just ain't worked out."

"We just ain't too good at raising money," Emil said.

Steve slammed his pencil on the desk. "We can't give up now. We can't let those crooks shoot that poor fox. We got to keep trying to get some money to buy that trap."

"How?" Arnold asked. "We tried everything so far, even getting jobs. Nothing worked out."

"I know, I know," Steve said tapping his pencil on the table. "But we can't give up now."

Emil shook his head. "We ain't got much choice."

Arnold nodded, his Adams Apple bouncing up and down. "Emil's right. We might as well forget about buying a trap and catching that fox."

"Why don't we just go back to the woods and chase the fox out," Emil suggested.

Steve shook his head. "Wouldn't work. We'd chase him around in those woods all Summer."

Just then, Boris came in grinning. He sat at the table, pulled out a candy bar, peeled the wrapper back and took a big bite out of it. Between bites and chewing and spraying candy, he grinned at the other boys.

Emil kept wiping the candy crumbs off the table. "Boris, you're a slob. Chew with your mouth closed. Stop spraying that stuff all over the place."

Arnold pointed to the door. "If you're gonna eat like a hog, go outside so we don't have to watch."

Boris wrapped up what was left of the candy bar. He stuck it in his pocket. He got up. "Ok, smart guys. You don't want to hear my good news, I'll go outside."

He started toward the door still grinning. Emil grabbed him by one arm and Arnold by the other. They pulled him back into his chair.

Emil smacked him on the shoulder with the back of his hand. "What good news?"

"If it is good news, it'll be the first we heard in awhile," Arnold said.

Boris reached into his pocket. He plopped a hand full of dimes and nickels on the table. "That's the good news. There's more where this came from."

The three boys stared at the pile of coins.

"Where did you steal this money?" Steve asked.

Boris had an injured look on his face. "I did not steal this money. Boris the Great does not steal. You guys are looking at Boris the Great, the next big show producer in America."

The three boys stared at Boris. Steve shook his head. "He robbed a bank. We'll all be thrown in jail for having a bank robber in our club."

Emil got up. "I'm getting out of here before the cops come after him."

Arnold jumped off his chair. "Me too."

Before the two boys could take a step, the door slammed open. A big girl rushed in followed by a group of other neighborhood hood girls who crowded the doorway. She had a mean grin on her face as she stood in front of the table, legs spread, both hands on her hips. She looked around the room. She pointed at the two chairs and then at Emil and Arnold. "You two clowns sit down and I mean sit down now."

Emil and Arnold wasted no time in plopping back into their chairs.

The clubhouse was real quiet as the big girl looked around with that mean grin still on her face. Several of the girls behind her giggled.

Steve recovered from the surprise of the girls barging into the clubhouse. He pointed at the big mean looking girl. "Can't you read? The sign outside says no girls allowed."

She shifted her mean grin to Steve. "It does does it. Well, I'm just gonna change it right now to read girls allowed."

Steve stood up. "You can't do that. This is private property. You are trespassing. You are breaking the law according to the United States Constitution, Section Four, Article . . ."

The big girl pointed at Steve. "Shut up and sit down you four eyed squirt."

Steve opened his mouth, closed it and sat down.

"Now that was a good idea Shorty for you to shut up and sit down." She looked at each boy in turn drilling them with her stare. "Which one of you cabbage heads calls yourself Boris the Great?'

Steve, Emil and Arnold pointed to Boris. "Him," they all said at the same time.

She focused on Boris who by now had a concerned look on his face.

"I should have known it was him. The girls told me it was the fat guy with the dumb look on his face."

While she talked, Boris was sliding the money off the table. The big girl pointed to the few coins left on the table. "Put em back on the table Fatso or I'll bust your head wide open."

Boris hesitated too long. She reached over the table, grabbed him by the shirt front with both hands and yanked him out of his seat right across the table through the coins. She put him in a headlock giving him a couple of good squeezes.

"Ow, ouch," Boris gasped. "That smarts."

The big girl turned the moaning groaning Boris around a couple of times to show Emil, Arnold and Steve. "This is what will happen you dummies do something like what Fatso tried." She gave Boris's head a couple of hard squeezes then shoved him away. "Sit down and shut up Boris the Great."

She moved closer to the table. "You guys listen real good. I'm only saying this one time. There ain't gonna be no girly show here. The girls ain't showing their underwear to any bunch of slobbering creeps you weird jerks are charging to see the show." She pointed to the coins scattered over the table and on the floor. She shook a fist at Boris. "You, Fatso, Boris the Great, pick up those coins, and hand em over. I'm cancelling your girly show right now. Those idiots will get their money back. You slobs will never ever have another girly show. Anybody pays you for one, I bust their heads and yours too. You creeps understand me?"

The three boys nodded as Boris scurried around on his hands and knees under the table picking up coins. He handed the coins to the big girl. He gave her a weak smile. "Here you are Sir."

She grabbed him into a ferocious headlock again saying, "I ain't no Sir. My name is Sylvia. You sniveling creeps better call me by my right name or you'll get what I'm giving Boris the Great."

She squeezed the gasping Boris/s head a few times then pushed him away. She moved closer to the table. The boys leaned back as if they were afraid she was going to reach across after them. Behind her, more girls were looking in through the door giggling.

Boris sat down rubbing his head. Emil, Arnold and Steve were staring at him. He avoided their eyes. Steve looked at Sylvia. "What girly show? We don't know anything about a girly show."

"You don't huh?" she pointed to Boris saying. "Why don't you ask Boris the Great, the big producer about it."

Boris never looked up. "I was just trying to help out, raise some money to save the fox." Sylvia gave out with a mean laugh. "He sure was. He promised the girls that maybe they would get to join your miserable club if they came here tomorrow night and showed their underwear to that bunch of sniveling snot nosed rats. Then, Boris the Great went around the neighborhood charging them a nickel to come see the girly show."

She leaned over and smacked the table in front of Boris real hard. "Ain't that right Boris the Great, the big producer of girly shows?"

Boris never looked up from the table as he rubbed his head and nodded.

Sylvia grinned. "Just for that, I made a new rule for this club. Any of the girls in the neighborhood who wants to can join this club. Instead of the Mound Street Tigers, you low life worms should have called it The Mound Street Pussy Cat Club."

Steve leaped to his feet. He waved his hand in the air. "That's illegal. This is private property. We are a Private club. You are in violation of the Constitution of the . . ."

That's as far as he got. Sylvia leaned over, grabbed him by the shirt front and yanked him across the table. She put him into a headlock and gave him a couple of noogies with her knuckles on his head then pushed him away.

"That's for talking when you should be listening and for threatening the new President of this lousy club."

The four boys stared at her. "You can't . . ." Arnold started to say then thought better of it when Sylvia doubled up her fists then took a step toward him. He never finished the sentence.

Sylvia grinned. "Shutting up was a smart move for you Eagle Beak."

She glared at each one of them, then gave them a wicked smile.

"Oh yeah, I almost forgot to mention it but you scummy creeps are kicked out of this club as of right now. We're taking over. I just elected myself President. The new name of this club is the Mound Street Daisies. That is, after we clean up this crummy joint."

Emil, Arnold and Boris glanced at Steve who looked straight ahead and shrugged his shoulders.

Sylvia stepped to one side. She motioned toward the door, "Now, you smelly dopes can leave right now or I bust your heads one at a time."

The four boys scrambled to their feet and bolted to the door with Boris leading. Sylvia aimed a kick at Emil before he made it out the door.

The boys walked away with Emil rubbing his butt. Sylvia stood in the door watching them go.

"And don't even think about snooping around here," she yelled.

Chapter 23

The next morning the boys met at the corner store. They all sat on the big yellow milk bottle storage boxes. No one said anything for awhile as each boy was deep in his own thoughts. Boris broke the long quiet spell. "I thought it was a good way to raise money. Remember, we did it last Summer. We made three dollars."

"Yeah, but last Summer there was no Sylvia living in the neighborhood," Emil said.

"There sure is now," Arnold added.

Steve just sat on the box shaking his head. "You did it again Boris. You almost got us killed, you got the crooks after us and now we don't have a clubhouse."

Boris jumped up. "Oh yeah, what about you guys?"

Emil pulled Boris into his chair. "Shut up and sit down. You done caused us enough trouble Boris the Great."

"I figured something was up when I saw her talking to the girls yesterday," Arnold said.

Steve sighed. "I guess it had to happen sooner or later."

"What we doing about a clubhouse?" Boris asked.

"We'll get ours back," Steve said.

"How?" Arnold asked.

"I'm thinking about it."

"What about our stuff still in there?" Emil asked.

Boris slid off the box. "I don't know about you guys, but I'm going over there right now and getting my magazines back."

"You mean the ones you just about wore out looking at the underwear ads?" Emil said.

"You're a real funny guy Emil," Boris said.

Arnold shook his head. "I'm not going near that place, I like my head just the way it is."

"They'll probably throw the stuff out where we can get it so why risk getting beat up by that Amazon?" Steve said.

Boris danced around using fancy footwork and jabbing at the air. "I ain't afraid. Bring her on. I'll murderize her. I'm going over there and get my stuff."

"It's your funeral," Arnold said.

Emil jumped off his seat on the box. "Let's go over and watch the fun if Sylvia catches Boris around their clubhouse."

"Our clubhouse," Steve corrected him. "I'm not ready to give up yet."

He got off the big milk box. "Let's go over and get our stuff. If anybody's there, we'll just ask them if we can have it."

The four boys walked over to their old clubhouse. A new sign was over the door. Steve pointed to it and read "Mound Street Daisies."

"Our lives are over if those hill jacks up on Macy Street see that sign." Emil said.

Arnold pointed to the two front windows. "Curtains. They even put up curtains."

"And they got flowers in front where everybody can see em." Emil said.

Boris studied the curtained windows and the two flower pots on each side of the door. "Makes the old clubhouse look kind of homey."

Steve read the rest of the wording on the sign: "Private Club girls only. No Trespassing. No Boys Allowed Specially low life creeps like Four Eyes Steve, Boris the Great Fatso, Skinny Big Honker Arnold and Ugly Banana Legs Emil. Violators will be beat up, tortured, shot hanged by their heels so they won't feel too good when they go home." Signed, Sylvia James President."

Boris danced around throwing punches into the air. "She don't scare Boris the Great. I'll give her a right and a left and another right, kapow. Just like that."

"Well what we doin now? They didn't leave our stuff outside," Arnold said.

Boris went to the window and looked in. "They got it all piled up in a corner. I'm going in through the window to get it. I'll throw it out to you guys."

Steve shook his head. "Better not Boris. That's breaking and entering."

"Hah, you guys may be chicken but Boris the Great ain't."

He opened one of the windows and pulled himself up into it. Halfway in, he got stuck. "Hey you guys, give me a boost."

Just then Sylvia came around from behind the building followed by a bunch of girls. She had a triumphant look on her face as she waved a canoe paddle. "We thought you creeps would come sneaking around here." She looked at Boris's big behind sticking out of the window. She tapped it lightly with the canoe paddle.

"Hey, you guys cut that out. That ain't funny. I'm stuck, give me a push."

Sylvia had a big grin on her face as she took a baseball batters stance behind the wriggling Boris's read end.

"Sure, I'll give you a boost, a great big boost," she said.

When Boris head Sylvia's voice, he let out a yell and said, "I was just admiring your pretty curtains."

"Sure you were," Sylvia said as she took a big back swing and yelled, "Batter up." She took a mighty swing and connected right on Boris's butt.

"Ow, ouch, ow," he yelled but was pushed only a little farther in the window.

Sylvia smacked him again, this time pushing him all the way through the window. He let out a loud and painful yowl as he fell on the floor of the clubhouse.

"Home run," the girls clapped and cheered.

Sylvia bowed to the cheering girls. "Thank you, thank you my loyal fans."

She waved the big canoe paddle at the other boys. "Any of you creeps want to be next?"

The three boys shook their heads. They backed away from the clubhouse. Sylvia unlocked the front door. She went inside then came out dragging a moaning Boris who groaned and rubbed his butt with every step. She shoved him toward the other boys. "Here's your Boris the Great. He ain't too good at being a burglar."

She went back into the clubhouse. Boxes and bags of the Mound Street Tigers stuff came flying through the front door. Sylvia came out grinning and dusting off her hands. "Don't try breaking into our clubhouse again. I catch any of you mud cruds around here, you won't like what happens to you." She motioned to the boxes and bags. "Now pick up your trash and get out of here."

Boris stumbled past the other boys then limped away still rubbing his butt. Emil, Arnold and Steve picked up the bags and boxes and followed Boris back to Choska's store.

Chapter 24

The next morning Emil, Arnold and Steve walked to Choska's store and sat on the milk bottle storage boxes waiting for Boris.

"Uh, oh," Arnold said pointing down the street. "Here they come."

Jimmy the Cheese's battered Cadillac turned the corner and parked by the side of the store where the boys were sitting. Bosco was driving. He got out and walked around to the passenger side where he glanced around in a guarded way. He looked in an open back window.

"Ok, Boss. All clear."

Usual opened the door for Jimmy who struggled to get his hefty bulk out of the back seat. Jimmy stood for a moment looking around, straightened his necktie then motioned with a nod of his head for the two men to follow him into Choska's store. He stopped when he saw the three boys and held out a hand for Bosco and Usual to wait. He stared long and hard at the three boys who never looked back at him. He shook his head.

"What a goofy looking bunch of kids."

The three men laughed as Bosco held the door open and the men went inside the store.

Mr. Choska was behind the counter when they came in.

Jimmy waved a hand at him. "Hey Choska, how you doing buddy?"

Choska eyed the three men and only nodded.

Jimmy leaned over the counter. He tapped Mr. Choska on the cheek with his open hand. "Is that the way to say hello to a business friend?"

Mr. Choska had a worried look on his face. "I don't need no more of your stuff. I don't want to sell your bootleg whiskey. It's against the law. I don't want to get in trouble with the law. I don't want to go to jail."

Jimmy shook his head. "Choska, Choska, how many times I got to tell you. You ain't getting in no trouble with the law. Those guys are friends of mine. You might say business partners." Jimmy turned to Bosco and Usual.

"Ain't that right boys?" Bosco and Usual laughed. "Yeah, yeah, business partners," Bosco said.

"Now Choska, you got to level with me. You ain't been buying from us until my two associates came in and got an order from the Mrs. What's going on? You buying stuff from somebody else? Huh, huh?"

Mr. Choska, a small man with a tiny well trimmed moustache, and slicked back hair, stared at the three men with hostile eyes, his face set in a hard expression. "I ain't buying nothing from nobody else and I ain't buying no more of your lousy stuff either. It almost killed me last week. I been telling everybody about how bad your stuff is. They'll be paralyzed and go blind they drink it."

Jimmy nodded. "Yeah, I been hearing that. You got some bad stuff out of that new still we set up after the other got blown up. We figured a weasel crook whose trying to muscle in here put something in our stuff made you sick."

Jimmy had a sympathetic look on his face. "I'll tell you what I'm going to do. I ain't charging you for two more jugs we're delivering today along with the order Mrs. Choska gave us the other day."

He made a slight motion with his head to Bosco and Usual. They left the store, went out to Jimmy's car and came back with four jugs of bootleg whiskey.

Jimmy smiled at Mr. Choska. "Now you see Choska, I don't hold no hard feelings. We'll just go along with business like, like usual." Jimmy laughed. He nudged Usual. "Ain't that a good one Usual? We're gonna do business like usual."

Bosco and Usual laughed.

Usual nudged Mr. Choska with his elbow. "Ain't that a good one Choska. Jimmy sure is one funny guy."

Mr. Choska's shoulders slumped. He shook his head.

Bosco slapped Jimmy on the shoulder. "You're a real comedian Boss."

Boris came out the back door of the family's living quarters behind the store. He rubbed his sore butt as he limped around to the side of the store where the other boys were. He pointed to the store. "Those three crooks are in there making my Dad take more of their bootleg whiskey. He could go to jail if the cops find it here."

Steve put a hand on Boris's shoulder. "Don't worry pal. Soon as they leave, we'll throw the stuff away."

Boris glanced to see that no one was coming out the side door. He lowered his voice. "Let's give those guys something to keep them busy."

"What?" Arnold asked.

Boris grinned. "I got a great idea." He limped behind the store into a storage shack. He came back and showed the other boys the can of flooring tile glue and a couple of old brushes. "Let's stick it to them."

Steve grinned. "Ok, Boris, since you're still hurting from those whacks Sylvia gave you, keep an eye on the door while we spread this stuff."

Emil, Steve and Arnold spread the flooring tile glue from the side door all the way to Jimmy's Cadillac. They finished just in time as Boris whispered. "Here they come."

Emil, Arnold and Steve ran behind the store into a stand of bushes in the back yard where they could watch. Boris limped after them barely making it into the bushes when the side door opened.

Bosco came out of the store first. He looked around, then, poked his head back into the store. "All clear Boss." He stepped to one side and held the door. Usual came out of the store next, looked around, then, stepped aside as Jimmy the Cheese followed. He stepped onto the sidewalk, looked around, straightened his tie, shrugged his shoulders then stepped into the thick layer of flooring tile glue that was already setting up. He tried to take a step. He stood looking down at his shoes.

Bosco looked up and down the street, then, still glancing around, stepped onto the sidewalk bumping into the stuck Jimmy. Bosco tried to lift his feet out of the adhesive. Usual, looking around, stepped onto the sidewalk and bumped into the stuck Bosco and Jimmy the Cheese. The three men fell into the sticky adhesive. They wallowed around as they kept trying to get up.

Mr. and Mrs. Choska heard the men yelling as they fought to get up out of the sticky mess. They rushed to the door and looked out. Mrs. Choska laughed. Mr. Choska pulled her back into the store and closed the door. "We got enough trouble with those guys. Don't make it no worse by laughing at them."

Bosco and Usual pulled Jimmy to his feet. The three men slogged their way to the car, got in and drove away. Jimmy was in the back seat yelling, "It was him. It was Icepick. I'll get him for this."

Chapter 25

Emil and Arnold went to the corner the next morning. Steve was reading a newspaper. He looked up. "Where's Boris?"

Both boys shrugged. "He should have been here already," Arnold said.

"He wasn't feeling too good from those whacks that Amazon Sylvia gave him." Emil said. "After those crooks got stuck in the glue he said he was going right to bed."

Steve put down the paper. "I'm worried. You think we should tell his Ma and Pa so they can take him to a Doctor?"

Arnold shook his head. "Nah. I asked him about that. He didn't want to go. Said his parents couldn't afford a Doctor since they have to buy that rotten bootleg whiskey from Jimmy the Cheese."

"Poor guy thinks he's dying," Emil said.

"He told me his butt hurts so bad they'll have to bury him upside down," Arnold said.

Steve tapped an ad in the newspaper. "I think this is our answer." He turned the page so they could see it.

Emil pointed to the ad. "What can some Preacher do to help our buddy?"

Arnold held up a hand as he read the ad. "Wait a minute Emil. This guy is one of those Preachers what claims he heals people."

Steve tapped the ad. "It says he heals the lame and the sick by laying on of the hands. He's what they call a Faith Healer."

Arnold rubbed his chin. "Well, Boris sure is lame and sick."

Emil studied the ad for a long moment. He looked at Steve and Arnold. "You guys think this guy can heal our buddy's butt?"

Steve shrugged. "It can't hurt to try."

Arnold read some more in the ad. "It says he got a tent revival and healing service tonight."

"Let's take Boris down there, let that Preacher heal him," Emil said.

"Ok, we'll do it," Steve said.

That evening the three boys met at Choska's grocery store. Boris came out limping, holding his butt and moaning with every step. "Hi you guys. I think I'm dyin. That Sylvia done killed me. I just came out to say goodbye to my good buddies." He tried to sit on one of the boxes. "Ow, ouch, ow, my butt hurts too much to sit down. I'll just go back inside, lay down on my stomach and wait to die." He hobbled toward the door. He turned and gave a weak wave. "So long good buddies. I may not make it through the night."

Steve jumped off his box. "Wait Boris. We got an idea that can heal you."

Boris listened while the boys explained they would take him to the revival where the evangelist would heal him.

Later, Steve, Arnold and Emil helped Boris walk to the old circus grounds where the revival tent was pitched. Arnold and Emil were on each side of Boris holding him up while he limped down the aisle moaning and groaning with every step as he followed Steve toward a front row seat. They walked the limping moaning Boris past people seated waiting for the service to begin.

Old ladies shook their heads and clucked in sympathy as they watched Boris limp past. He saw them looking at him and heard their clucking so he really laid it on. He moaned louder with each feeble step that became more feeble with each moan. Each step threatened to be his last as Emil and Arnold held him up.

"Hang in there old Buddy," Emil said.

"The good Preacher will heal you. Have faith," Arnold said. "Have faith."

Boris moaned louder and longer as the boys helped him to a seat in front of the raised platform where the Reverend was to conduct the service. He gave out a loud moan as he sat down. His head lolled to one side as he kept on giving off small moans then every so often letting out with a big one as he shifted his position on the chair.

Steve went to the back of the tent where he talked to the Reverend Benson's assistants.

One of them laid a hand on Steve's shoulder. "We'll have the Reverend heal your friend first and get him out of his misery," he said in a deep somber voice that would have fit well in a funeral home.

Steve shook his hand saying, "Thank you sir. Thank you. You'll be helping our friend get his life back."

Steve hurried back to the front of the tent and sat where the moaning Boris was between Emil and Arnold who were propping him up.

Several old ladies got up and came over to Boris. They leaned over him clucking and shaking their heads. One of the old ladies put a hand on Boris's shoulder. Another one patted his head.

"Have faith young man, have faith," the first old lady said as she patted his shoulder.

"The good Reverend Benson will heal you. Just have faith," the other old lady said as she patted his head.

Boris raised his head, looked at the lady and gave out with a louder than usual moan then said, "Thank you, thank you," in a weak voice then his head lolled to one side again.

The other old lady patted Boris's shoulder. "There, there young man. Have faith. The Lord works in wondrous ways."

One of the ladies turned to Emil. "What is wrong with this nice young man?"

"He got hit in the butt."

"Yeah, now he's got some horrible disease in his butt," Arnold said.

The two old ladies jerked their hands away from Boris's head and shoulders. "Aagh," one of them said as she hurried back to her seat.

The other old lady stared at Boris. "Ugh, how awful," she said as she went to her seat. Both old ladies kept pointing to Boris and telling other old ladies around them what they just heard. There was much clucking and shaking of heads as people seated on either side of the boys and behind them got up and moved to other seats several rows away from Boris.

Within a few minutes, an organ began playing. A big man in his mid fifties with a bulging stomach wearing a snow white suit bounded down the aisle to the stage shouting in a deep voice "Praise the Lord, Praise the Lord." His heavy fleshy face was red from the exertion of bounding down the aisle. Sweat glistened off his face and strands of long hair he had combed sideways over the bald spot on his head were dancing in the breeze created by several big fans.

People in the audience were standing up and shouting, "Praise the Lord, Praise the Lord."

The Reverend Benson danced a jig on the stage then raised his hands for the congregation to be quiet and seated.

When the people were seated and quiet, the Reverend Benson raised his arms again. "This is a great evening. We'll start our healing service with a young man who has been brought here by his friends. He is in great pain and could pass away at any time, any time. This young man will be healed tonight right here in front of you. Praise the Lord."

The congregation stood and began chanting, "Praise the Lord, Praise the Lord."

The Reverend Benson motioned them to sit down. He looked at Boris, then at Emil and Arnold. He beckoned to them with outstretched arms.

"Bring your sick young friend who is afflicted by a horrible disease and is in terrible pain. Bring him here where I can lay hands on him. He will be healed. He will be healed. It is the will of the Good Lord that this young man will be healed through me who is the instrument of his will."

Steve led Emil and Arnold who were supporting the limping staggering groaning Boris who was now moaning louder than ever up onto the stage where the Reverend waited. When Boris was in front of him, he raised his left hand. He put his right hand on Boris's forehead then closed his eyes and talked faster and faster.

Arnold leaned toward Steve. "What's he saying?"

Steve stared fascinated at the Preacher. "He's talking in tongues."

"What's that?" Emil asked.

"Some kind of religious babbling when a Preacher gets all charged up." Steve said.

"Now, now," thundered the Reverend in his deep booming voice, his eyes still closed, "I lay my hands on this young man's afflicted painful part of his body so he will be healed, healed."

Boris stared at the Preacher. He shrugged his shoulders and turned around. The Reverend's hands slid down Boris's shoulders then to his back. Boris bent over. The Reverend's hands slide down his back until they landed on Boris's huge butt. With his eyes still closed, the Reverend began squeezing Boris's butt cheeks while shouting louder than ever, "Heal, heal, heal."

"I'm getting healed, I'm getting healed, I'm getting healed," Boris yelled. "Don't stop now Reverend. I'm getting healed."

Surprised by Boris's sudden outburst, the Reverend opened his eyes. He saw that he had been squeezing Boris's butt checks. He jerked his hands away and let out a roar of outrage. Boris straightened and began dancing around the stage waving his arms in the air. "I'm healed, I'm healed."

The enraged Reverend started after Boris yelling, "You won't be healed when I get through with you."

Boris dodged the enraged Preacher's charge that took him off the stage into the audience. Boris was off the stage and running up the aisle followed by Emil, Arnold and Steve. The audience was in an uproar as the shouting, swearing Reverend tried to get up out of the tangle of chairs and people. The old ladies were grabbing at him yelling, "Praise the Lord, you healed him, you healed him."

With the now healed Boris leading, the boys ran out of the tent. Down the road they could still hear the Reverend Benson yelling, "I'll kill him, I'll kill him."

Boris pulled far ahead of the others. He was yelling as he ran, "I'm healed, I'm healed. Praise the Lord."

The next morning, Steve, Arnold and Emil met at Choska's store.

"You guys seen Boris yet this morning?" Steve asked.

Arnold shook his head.

"He's probably halfway to California by now the way he was running," Emil said.

"Good thing," Arnold said, "the way that Preacher was yelling he was gonna kill him."

Boris poked his head out the side door. He looked around. "Anybody out here looking for me?"

"Nobody yet," Emil said.

"Great," Boris said. He came out and danced around punching the air. "I'm healed, I'm healed."

Steve looked around. "Not so loud Boris. That Preacher may come looking for you."

Boris grinned. "No way. One of the customers in the store said the Reverend folded his tent, left town last night, said everybody in this town is crazy."

Chapter 26

Jimmy the Cheese, Bosco and Usual are in the poolroom drinking coffee and eating donuts. Bosco made loud slurping noises as he drank his coffee.

Jimmy gave him an irritated look. "You got to slurp like a hog when you drink that coffee?"

Bosco put half a donut into his mouth. "It's good stuffs Boss."

"You got any ideas about what we can do about that crook Icepick?" Usual asked.

Jimmy shook his head. "I'm still working on it."

Bosco slurped some more coffee. He stuffed the other half of the donut in his mouth. "It's been pretty quiet for a couple of days."

Jocko hurried down the stairs into the poolroom. "You guys hear about what happened last night at the big revival tent at the Circus Grounds?"

Bosco and Usual ignored Jocko and kept on eating donuts and drinking coffee like there was never any more going to be made.

Jimmy shook his head. "What? What happened last night?"

Jocko went to the coffee pot. He poured a cup, grabbed a couple of donuts and sat at his desk behind the counter.

Bosco watched him. "Hey, you took two donuts."

Jocko took a big bite out of one. He pointed to an empty box. "So what? You and Usual musta eat a dozen of em already."

Usual poured another cup of coffee. He looked at Jocko. "Oh yeah. Well, we got to keep our strength up. We work all day not like you sitting here all day shuffling papers."

Jimmy smacked the table. "Will you guys shut up for just one minute. Ok. Jocko, what happened at that revival last night?"

Jocko kept biting and chewing on a donut and slurping coffee in between bites. He wagged a finger at Jimmy. "I'm telling you Jimmy, you wouldn't believe what went down right there in that revival tent while that Preacher was having a healing service."

Jimmy glared at Jocko. "If you ain't telling me what happened, I'm having Bosco beat it out of you."

Bosco started to get up. "That's a great idea Boss."

Jocko raised his hands. "All right, all right, I'm telling you what happened."

Jocko finished the last of his two donuts and downed his coffee in one big gulp. He wiped his mouth with his sleeve. "I was there. I saw it with my own eyes I did."

Jimmy's face started turned red. "Saw what? Saw what?"

Jocko put up a hand. "I'm getting to that."

"Well get to it now," Jimmy's tone was menacing.

Jocko swallowed the last of his donut. "Ok, ok. This Reverend, this guy what claims he can heal peoples when they're sick, he went crazy last night. He went so crazy he chased some guys right out of that revival tent."

Jimmy moved one hand in a circling motion for Jocko to go on.

Jocko poured another cup of coffee. "There was these four guys, these four guys who came in the tent. One of them was sick, you know moaning, groaning, wobbling sick, so sick he was helped to the stage by two other funny looking guys while a midget wearing coke bottle glasses cleared the way through the crowd to the stage."

Jocko drank more coffee. He looked in the bag for another donut. He rooted around till he found a big jelly filled one. He stared at it for a long moment.

"Then what, then what?' Jimmy said waving a hand.

Jocko took a bite out of the last donut. He chewed hard for a moment, drank some more coffee. "This moaning, groaning sick wobbly fat guy with the black bushy hair who could barely walk was up on the stage."

Jimmy jumped up out of his chair. He cut Jocko off. "Wha'd you say" A fat guy with black bushy hair?"

Bosco and Usual stared at Jocko with their mouths open. "Bushy haired fat guy," they said at the same time.

Bosco was enjoying being the center of attention. He swilled more coffee. "Yeah. A fat guy with black bushy hair. He was so sick he could hardly walk. Those two funny looking guys had to hold him up for that Preacher to heal him."

Jocko paused for effect, then continued when he saw irritation flash over Jimmy's face. "This Preacher, a real big guy in one of those white suits you see at Easter, put his hands on that sick moaning groaning fat bushy haired guy's head, closed his eyes and yelled and hollered and mumbled in some kind of foreign language I ain't never heard before and kept yelling something about heal, heal."

More coffee, another bite of a donut, then Jocko went on. "He turned the sick fat bushy haired guy around and began rubbing his shoulders and pounding on em still hollering and yelling in that funny sounding foreign language, heal this sinner, heal this sinner." Then, that sick fat bushy haired moaning groaning fat buy bends over. His two buddies catch him to keep him from hittin the floor. The yelling, hollering Preacher yelling and hollering in that foreign language I never heard before had his eyes closed. He never noticed that sick fat moaning groaning bushy haired guy was bending over. His hands slid down to the sick fat bushy haired guy's big butt where that hollering and yelling Preacher with his eyes closed started hollering and yelling heal, heal while he squeezed that sick fat guy's big fat butt.

Jocko paused again for another drink of coffee. "He must have not known he was squeezing this fat guy's butt cause he had his eyes closed. That fat guy was moaning and groaning at first, then he looked around at the Reverend rubbing his butt and began yelling, 'That feels great Reverend don't stop, don't stop. I'm getting healed, I'm getting healed.' Then, the Reverend opened his eyes. He saw he wasn't rubbing the fat kid's shoulders. He was rubbing this fat guy's butt. The fat guy began jumping around on the stage yelling I'm healed. I'm healed. That Reverend at first looked like he lost his voice. Then he found it. Boy, did he find it. He let out a yell that must have been heard two miles away. He started after that fat guy yelling he was gonna kill him dead. But, that fat guy saw him coming. He had a good head start on that Preacher. He jumped off the stage. His three buddies jumped right after him. They all ran up the aisle with that Preacher hollering and swearing something awful, stumbling around on the stage shaking his fists at em. He jumped off the stage but missed the steps. He fell right onto a bunch of screaming old ladies in the front row. He got all tangled up in chairs and old ladies who were trying to hug him. They was all yelling Praise the Lord, Praise the Lord while they all pawed at the Reverend Preacher trying to get a good hold on him to give him a hug or something."

Jocko took a deep breath. He looked in the empty donut bag. He faked a shiver. He leaned back in his chair. "It wasn't a pretty sight. I can tell you that."

Jimmy the Cheese, Bosco and Usual stared at Jocko. Jimmy shook his head. "What kind of crook is that guy Icepick stirring things up in a church?

"A revival tent not a church," Jocko interrupted.

"Same thing," Jimmy said.

Bosco clucked. "What a low down dirty rotten thing for a crook to do in a church yet."

Jocko pointed at him. "A tent not a ch . . ."

"Shut up," Jimmy yelled.

Usual kept shaking his head. "What a lousy thing to do. A guy like Icepick gives all mobsters a bad name."

Jimmy thought for a moment. He nodded with a knowing look on his face toward Bosco and Usual. "You guys must have winged that fat bushy haired guy."

"Boy, that Reverend Preacher sure must a been some healer to make that fat bushy haired guy well after taking a load of buck shot in the butt." Jocko said.

Jimmy agreed. "Cheaper'n going to a doctor."

"What we doing about Icepick Boss? You got that plan worked out yet?" Usual asked.

Jimmy thought for a moment before answering. "I been thinking."

Bosco leaned toward Jimmy. "Yeah, yeah Boss, you been thinking."

Not to be outdone, Usual leaned closer to Jimmy. "What you been thinking Boss?"

"I been thinking," Jimmy said as he stared past them as though deep in thought. "That Icepick knows our every move. Every which way we turn that guy is way ahead of us to screw things up like he does."

Both Bosco and Usual nodded.

Bosco turned to look at Jocko. "I think you hit it." Boss. "Maybe we got a spy in here what's been working for Icepick."

"Maybe we do," Jimmy said as the three men stared at Jocko.

Jocko look up. "What, what? What you guys staring at me for?"

"You know what happens to spies don't you Jocko?" Jimmy said.

Bosco grinned at Jocko. "They get a brand new pair of cement overshoes. That's what they get."

"Yeah," Usual said, "that's after they try on their new cement pajamas."

Jocko looked at the three staring at him. "You guys are kidding me right? You guys are mad at me because I ate four donuts aintcha?"

Usual held up five fingers. "Five."

"Ok, ok maybe it was five but I ain't no spy. Tell these guys Jimmy. I been working right here when all that stuff happened to them. Tell em."

Jimmy gave a weary nod. "Yeah, yeah. Jocko's been right here working all the time."

Jocko flipped the sweat off his forehead. "Maybe you guys been drinking too much of that stuff you're makin out at the farm. Maybe you guys are talking too much around town. Maybe that Icepick ain't so dumb. He's been outsmarting you guys every which way."

Bosco started to get up with both fists clenched.

Jimmy motioned with his hands. "Sit down Bosco. Maybe he's right. Maybe that guy is just outsmarting us at every turn. Maybe we ain't been too careful about watching our backs better." Usual sat back listening. He wagged a finger toward Jimmy. "You ever think about somebody else? Somebody who always seems to be around when things happen? Somebody what maybe Icepick is paying off to do his dirty work for him?"

Jimmy perked up. His eyes narrowed. "Who, who?"

Bosco stared at Usual. "You don't mean . . . . ?"

Usual nodded. "Those funny looking kids what hangs around up at Choska's store. Who else was there to put down that sticky stuff the other day? Who else was at the golf course? Who else always is always around when something happens?"

"Those funny looking kids," Jimmy and Bosco said at the same time.

"I been thinking about that fat bushy haired guy. You guys ever take a good look at Choska's kid, fat bushy haired just like we think Icepick looks like in a disguise," Usual said.

Jimmy shook his head. "We all agreed Choska's kid was too dumb looking to be Icepick in disguise."

"Yeah, he ain't even bushy haired no more. Plasters his hair down," Usual said.

"A master of disguise, that Icepick," Jimmy said.

There was a long silence as the three men stared at the table. Jocko looked up several times from his calculator relieved that he appeared to be off the hook for being suspected of spying for Icepick. If these cheese heads ever found out he really was planted in here by Uncle Junie to keep an eye on them and that goofy nephew of his who goes around calling himself Icepick Pete like he was a real bad guy, they may get the wrong idea and still give him that cement underwear or cement pajamas. He busied himself trying to remember what it was they said they'd give him if he was a spy for Icepick.

Chapter 27

The next morning Emil, Arnold and Steve were sitting outside of Choska's store. Emil broke the silence, "that wasn't such a good idea taking Boris to see that healing Preacher."

"What do you mean? It worked didn't it? Boris's butt got healed," Arnold said.

"Classic case of mind of matter," Steve said.

"Yeah sure, Boris's mind didn't matter."

"Steve, why don't you talk English for once," Emil said.

Arnold pointed a thumb toward Steve. "I know what he means. He means you use your mind then the hurt don't matter."

"Something like that," Steve said. Boris came out of the store. He danced around jabbing the air with rights and lefts as he went in to his boxers routine. "They can't keep Boris the Great down."

A battered old car stopped at the curb near where the boys were sitting and Boris was punching the air and dancing around. A short heavy set man got out. He wore a Cleveland Indians baseball cap, a white sweat shirt and baggy sweat pants that looked like they held up his belly that spilled over the top. An unlit cigar jutted out one side of his mouth. His fleshy round face was red from the effort of just getting out of his car. He stopped and with his hands on his hips watched Boris go though his boxing routine. Now that he had more of an audience, Boris added more fancy footwork and a couple of uppercut punches.

The short heavy set man folded his arms across his chest as he watched and nodded approval. He took the cigar stub out of his mouth. "You ever do any fighting boy?"

Boris let go with a few more jabs. He stopped. He looked at the short fat man. "No sir. But Boris the Great ain't afraid of nobody." He jabbed the air a couple more times.

The short man shook his head. "Nah, I don't mean street fighting. You ever do any boxing, you know, like this?" He went into a boxing stance. He shuffled around throwing punches. He put the cigar stub back into a corner of his mouth. He took it out again and jabbed it at Boris. "Ya know what I mean kid?"

Boris stared at the man. "Yes sir, I mean no sir."

He pointed at Boris. "Yessiree. I see the makings of a world champeen fighter standing right there, a guy who could be making big bucks. Yessiree, you got real potential Kid."

Boris stared at him. "You, you really think so sir. You really think I could be a world champeen fighter and, and make big bucks. I got potential?"

"Yessiree bob. I think you got what it takes."

Boris turned to the other boys. "You guys hear that. I got potential. I could be a world champeen fighter. The man kept nodding as he looked Boris up and down. "With some good training, good handling, you could be on your way to the top Kid."

He moved closer to Boris. He felt his arms.

"Yep, you got em Kid. You got em. You got the arms of a fighter."

"I do?"

"Yeah kid. Only one in a million got it. Looks like you got it."

Boris stared at the short fat man. He bent his right arm up and felt his muscle. He bent his left arm up and felt that muscle.

The man stood back with his hands on his hips as he gave Boris an admiring look.

"I'm gonna be your manager Kid. I don't take on no stiffs. I only take on guys what got it. And you got it."

He pulled a pad out of the back pocket of his sweat pants. He wrote on it, tore off the sheet and handed it to Boris. "I got you booked for a fight Friday night at seven down at the gym under the Freestone Union Hall. You'll be on your way to the big time and big bucks, Kid, in no time at all. Be there."

The short fat man got in his car and drove off in a cloud of blue smoke while the boys and Boris watched it go. Boris raised his arms over his head in a victory salute, the way he saw them do in the movies. He danced around with the fanciest footwork the other boys had ever seen. He punched and feinted and ducked and crouched and threw uppercuts and looping over the top punches. He clasped his hands over his head the way he saw boxers do in the newsreels at the movies.

"I'm the champeen of the world. I'm makin big bucks."

The side door of the store opened. Boris's Mother looked out. "What's all the yelling about?"

Boris raised his arms. He executed a back pedal and crossover move.

"I'm gonna be champeen of the world. I'm gonna make big bucks."

"That's nice," his Mother said. "Now come in. I made you some nice chicken soup."

Boris went in the store. The door opened. He poked his head out. "You guys just watch. I'm gonna be champeen of the world."

Emil, Arnold and Steve looked at each other. Finally Steve said, "You guys know who that was?"

Emil and Arnold shook their heads.

"That was Punchy Malone."

"Punchy Malone. Who's he?" Arnold asked.

"Yeah, Punchy Malone," Emil said. "Now, I remember. My Dad told me about him. He used to be a fighter. He wasn't very good. He opened that boxing gym down on Main Street under the Union Hall near the Freestone plant. He works in the tire factory now. Has boxing shows there every Friday night."

"Why does he want Boris? He couldn't punch his way out of a paper bag," Arnold asked.

"He's out of shape. He won't last one minute," Emil said.

"I heard about how Punchy Malone runs his fights," Steve said. "He drags guys like Boris in, throws them against some boxer he's trying to build up. These guys get slaughtered and Punchy makes money from a bunch of goofs who like to watch and bet. Then he gives the loser a dollar and sends him on his way after they take him to the hospital."

Arnold got off the box. "Then we got to save Boris, not let him go there."

Steve shook his head. "Won't work. Boris don't show up, Punchy sends a couple guys after him. They'll rough him up and drag him to the gym.

"Boris's goose is cooked since he told that Malone guy he'd be there," Emil said.

"He shows up, he gets beat up. He doesn't show up, he gets beat up anyway," Emil said.

"How can we save our buddy?" Arnold asked.

"He's got to show up now or he's really in for it," Emil said.

Steve was quiet for a long moment.

"What?" Arnold asked.

"What, what?" Emil asked.

Steve had that thoughtful look on his face like he always had when he came up with an idea.

"Let's go down to Mr. Punchy Malone's gym. We'll find out who Boris has to fight and then . . ." Steve outlined his plan to Emil and Arnold.

"It just might work," Arnold said.

"It's worth a try," Emil said.

That evening, Steve, Emil and Arnold walked down the hill to the Freestone Union Hall. They went round to the back where a sign above a door said Malone's Gym. A faded arrow pointed down a flight of rickety stairs. The three boys went inside the gym. It smelled of sweat, liniment, wet leather and sweaty work out clothes. A boxing ring was in the center of the big room. Along each wall, several heavy punching bags and speed bags hung from the ceiling where young men and boys were hitting them. Two fighters were sparring in the ring while Punchy and several other men watched, occasionally shouting instructions to the two fighters. Other young men in sweat suits were jumping rope while several mor were shadow boxing. The three boys stood for awhile looking around the gym watching the two fighters sparring in the ring.

Arnold pointed to the boxing ring. "Why do they call it a ring when it's square?"

"Beats me," Emil answered.

Steve shrugged. "I don't know. I guess they call it that because when a fighter gets hit hard enough, his head rings."

Emil whispered to Steve. "What guy is Boris supposed to fight Friday night?"

Just then, Punchy Malone turned away from watching the two boxers in the ring. He yelled at a tall muscular kid hitting a heavy bag without much enthusiasm.

"Come on Sliwinski. Pick it up. You wanna beat that guy Boris the Great, don't ya?"

Punchy and the other men with him laughed. One of the men slapped him on the back saying. "Punchy, you're a real card. The only thing we got to worry about after Sliwinski gets done with that fat kid is what hospital we got to send him."

"You got it Boss," Sliwinski yelled back. He charged into the heavy bag with rights and lefts and more rights and lefts along with a dazzling display of footwork.

"Attaboy," Punchy yelled then turned back to watching the two kids sparring in the ring.

Emil, Steve and Arnold glanced at each other with worried looks on their faces. Steve made a slight motion with his head for Emil and Arnold to follow him as he walked over close to where the muscular fighter was hitting the heavy bag. Sliwinski stopped to wipe the sweat off his face.

"What do you think?" Steve said loud enough for Sliwinski to hear.

Arnold looked around as if he was checking to see no one was close to hear him. "Piece of cake," he said lowering his voice. "Boris the Great will kill that skinny Sliwinski kid."

At the mention of his name, Sliwinski turned around to see who was talking. The three boys ignored him and kept talking in lowered voices as Sliwinski moved closer going through the motions of shadow boxing.

Emil laughed. "Boris the Great could take that skinny guy Sliwinski with one hand tied behind his back."

"Yeah, it's a shame that Punchy Malone sends a kid like Sliwinski up against a pro like Boris the Great," Steve said.

Emil shook his head. "Cannon fodder. That's what that kid is going to be Friday night against a guy like Boris the Great who's got thirty straight knockouts."

Arnold shook his head. "Three of those guys are still in the hospital. There ought to be a law throwing kids like Sliwinski up against a meat grinder like Boris the Great."

By now, Sliwinski had a worried look on his face. He kept glancing at the three boys as he went back to making motions of hitting the heavy bag. He watched while the three boys laughed and threw fake punches at each other as they left the gym.

Outside the gym, the three boys stopped. Steve looked around first before talking. "What do you guys think." Did it work? Did we scare him?"

Emil nodded. "We got him thinking."

"And then some," Arnold said.

Steve laughed. "Ok, we got two more days before the fight. Let's go back each night, lay it on real thick. Let's get that guy so scared he'll be on his way to South America Friday night to get away from fighting that ferocious tiger Boris the Great."

"We shouldn't tell Boris what we're doing," Arnold said.

"Let's keep quiet about it," Emil said.

"We'll keep encouraging Boris to make sure he shows up Friday night," Steve said.

"Let's sure hope we got that Sliwinski guy so scared he doesn't show up or it's curtains for Boris the Great," Arnold said.

"Don't worry. We won't let Boris get in the ring with Sliwinski if he does show up," Steve said.

"I don't know. Boris is convinced he's a great fighter," Emil said. "It'll be tough keeping him out of that ring."

"We'll have to wait until Friday," Steve said. "We got our work cut out to scare the crap out of that guy Sliwinski."

For the next two days, Emil, Arnold and Steve watched Boris get ready for his first fight on his way to be champeen of the world. Boris shadow boxed for a couple of minutes, then went in to his Dad's store and came out with an ice cream cone. "Got to keep my strength up," he said. He kept up this routine a couple of times a day always following with a huge ice cream cone. Then, he would go in the house to take a nap. "Got to save my strength," he would say.

For the next two evenings, Steve, Arnold and Emil went to Punchy Malone's gym. Each time they repeated their performance of scaring Sliwinski. On the last night before the Friday night fight, the three gave it extra effort. Before they were finished building up Boris the Great as the toughest, meanest, greatest raw meat fighter since Jack Dempsey, the unraveled, shaken Slinwinski was even missing the heavy bag as he made sluggish attempts at hitting it.

Punchy Malone figured Sliwinski had a case of nerves about the coming fight just like all good fighters have, he told the other guys at the gym.

Friday, the night of Boris's big fight came. The four boys walked down to the gym under the Freestone Union Hall. The bouts were already under way when they got there. Every seat in the hall was full. The boys hurried the now nervous Boris into the cramped dressing room. They put tape on his hands just like the other fighters they saw had on theirs. Steve motioned Emil aside. He whispered, "Go out. See if Sliwinski showed up."

Emil came back in the dressing room. He shook his head. Steve and Arnold came over to him while Boris was dancing around jabbing the air. "Sliwinski is a no show. Punchy is yelling all over the place."

Steve and Arnold grinned. "It worked," Steve said. "Let's get Boris out there."

Boris got in the ring. He danced around, giving an exhibition of dazzling footwork. He punched the air. He jabbed, he uppercutted, he feinted, he crouched, he snarled menacingly. The crowd cheered him on. There was a hurried conference on one side of the ring in what was supposed to be Killer Sliwinski's corner. Finally, the referee came into the center of the ring. He motioned Boris over.

"Killer Sliwinski didn't show up for this here fight." He raised Boris's hand. "So, the winner is Boris the Great."

The crowd cheered as Boris danced around the ring with his taped hands clasped above his head like he saw boxers do in the movies. The referee called him to the center of the ring. Steve, Emil and Arnold jumped in and escorted Boris to the referee.

"What's gonna be your next fight?" The referee asked.

Steve nodded to Emil and Arnold who grabbed Boris's arms. They pulled him away from the referee. Steve stepped forward and said to the referee, "Boris the Great will retire undefeated. He wants to be a concert piano player so he has to protect his hands."

Emil and Arnold hustled the protesting Boris back into the dressing room. "What're you guys doing? I don't want to be no piano player. I won. I'm on the way to being champeen of the world and, and making big bucks."

Steve came in the dressing room. "Shut up Boris. We just saved your life. If Sliwinski showed up he would have killed you. He's a big mean kid in great shape who has been fighting for awhile. He just got out of reform school for beating up three guys in one fight."

"Yeah," Emil said. "We came over here for the last three nights and talked about how tough and mean you were, how many fights you won, how many guys you put in the hospital."

Boris's eyes were wide as he listened. "Thanks for saving my life you guys. Let's go home," he said in a quiet voice.

Chapter 28

Emil and Arnold were sitting on the big yellow milk storage boxes when Steve walked up and joined them. Boris came out of the side door a few minutes later. They all sat there for a few minutes without saying anything.

Finally, Emil broke the silence. "Well, what do we do now?"

"We still don't have our clubhouse back," Arnold said.

"Those two crooks are out there trying to kill the fox and Jimmy the Cheese is still making my Ma and Pa buy his rotten bootleg whiskey," Boris said.

"I know, I know," Steve said. "Things sure don't look too good right now. But we can't just give up. We got to save that little fox first then take care of the other things one at a time."

Emil shook his head. "We ain't been doing too good raising money for that trap to catch the fox."

"Why don't we just give it up, go swimming, enjoy our Summer," Arnold said.

Steve shook his head. "We can't just give it up. We got to keep going. We got to soldier on. We're the Mound Street Tigers. We see trouble, we help."

"Sounds great but we ain't doing too well being the Mound Street Tigers what helps with problems when we don't even have a clubhouse," Boris said.

Steve held up a hand. "First things first. We got to save that fox. It's in the most danger right now from being shot by those crooks."

"How?" Arnold asked.

"Yeah how?" Emil asked.

"You got any more great ideas?" Boris asked.

Steve raised one hand. "If you guys will shut up for a minute, I'll tell you about a plan I got." He outlined the plan for them. "What do you guys think?"

The three boys stared at Steve. "Are you nuts or something?" Emil said.

"How you figure on getting close enough to talk to Sylvia without her tearing your head off?" Arnold asked.

Boris laughed. "We'll watch your skull pop open when she grabs you in a headlock."

The three boys watched as Steve walked toward their old clubhouse.

Arnold shook his head. "If he pulls this off without getting his skull popped open, we ought to run him for President of the United States."

Just as Steve got to the clubhouse, Sylvia came out. She stood in front of Steve with her hands on her hips blocking his way.

"Why you hanging around here Shorty? Didn't I tell you guys to stay away if you knew what's good for you?"

Steve stepped back as she moved toward him with her fists clenched. He held his hands out toward her in a defensive position. "I'm not just hanging around here Sylvia. I came to tell you about something that can make you famous."

In one quick move, she had him in a headlock. "Oh yeah, and I can make you famous for having the skinniest head in town."

She looked up the street where Emil, Arnold, and Boris were watching. "You crum bums better get out of here or you all get the same thing," she yelled.

"I knew it. I knew it," Arnold said. "He's done for."

Boris turned and ran back toward the corner yelling, "She's gonna kill us. It's every man for himself."

Emil and Arnold were right behind him. Emil slowed. He looked back. He stopped. "Hey you guys, look."

Boris and Arnold stopped. They turned around and looked just as Sylvia put her arm around Steve's shoulder and guided him into the clubhouse.

Boris gasped. "She's going to kill him inside."

Emil grabbed Boris and Arnold by the arms. "Let's get out of here. She'll come after us next."

"We better wait, see if he needs a Doctor after she throws him out," Arnold said.

The boys waited. "It don't look good," Arnold said.

"She's probably torturing him before she rips his head off and throws him out," Boris said.

"Our good buddy is gone for good," Arnold said his voice trembling.

Boris was shaking his head and wringing his hands. "We tried to tell him. We tried."

Suddenly, Emil pointed toward the clubhouse. "Look, I don't believe it."

Steve and Sylvia came out of the clubhouse. She had her arm around his shoulder. She was smiling. She shook hands with Steve and went back inside the clubhouse.

Steve walked past the three boys. He stared straight ahead. "You guys wait for me at the store," he said out of the corner of his mouth and slowed his walk. The three boys hurried around the corner and waited at the store. Steve was whistling as he came around to where the three boys waited for him. When he came up to them, he did a little two step and punched the air a couple of times, then sat on one of the big milk bottle boxes.

"Wow, Boris said. "We didn't think you could pull it off."

"What did you say?" Emil asked.

"How did you do it?" Arnold asked.

"I said what I said, did what I did," Steve answered.

"What did you did?" Boris asked.

"I told you guys it was a piece of cake," Steve said.

"We thought she was going to tear your head off after she grabbed you," Arnold said.

"Boy, I had to talk fast to get her off my back," Steve said.

"What did you say to her? Boris asked.

"I told her she could be famous if she helped us in our drive to save the fox. At first, she thought I was nuts. I convinced her that the newspapers and radio stations would probably cover this great story about how she stepped in to help save the little fox from a horrible death at the hands of those two crooks. She'd get her picture in the paper. She'd be on the radio and everything. The Mayor and even the Governor would probably give her medals. Even the President would know about what she did to save the fox. He might even come here to give her a medal too."

"Wow," Boris said.

"Who'd thunk it?" Emil said.

"We never would thought in a million years you could pull it off," Arnold said.

"What happens now?" Emil asked.

"We start the drive tomorrow," Steve said. "The girls will make a bunch of save the red fox signs today so we got to be ready to go bright and early."

Boris went to a shed behind the store. He came back carrying the stiff dried out dead cat by the tail. He held it up. "Let's show Arthur to people, tell them this is what will happen to the red fox if we don't save it from being killed by those crooks."

Emil, Arnold and Steve backed away from Boris and the stiff, dried out cat.

"Oh yeah, and who's carrying it around out in the hot sun?" Arnold asked.

"Not me," Emil said.

"We don't have to carry it around," Boris said. "I got somebody else."

"Who?" Emil asked. "Are the girls going to do it?"

Boris grinned. "Naw, not the girls. Sylvia's little brother Mikey been pestering me about joining our club. I made a deal with him. He carries Arthur around when the girls go out to get donations, he gets in our club. We'll make him a Mound Street Tiger-sometime."

"What's he going to do with a dead cat?" Arnold asked.

Boris shook his head. "Boy, you guys got no imagination. When people answer the door, Sylvia tells them about saving the red fox. She'll tell them that this is what will happen to the red fox when those crooks shoot it if we don't save it. Then, Mikey holds up the dead cat. It can't miss. The girls will get donations every time."

Chapter 29

The next day the four boys were at the clubhouse where the girls were already busy hand painting Save the Red Fox signs. Sylvia spotted the four boys. She came over to them. She had her hands on her hips as she looked at each one of them then fastened on Steve. "Ok Shorty, what are you and your goofy buddies doing to help save the red fox, Huh, Huh?"

Steve gestured toward a table the girls had set up outside the clubhouse. "I'll make this table the headquarters for the drive. That way I'll be able to tell the newspaper reporters and radio guys where to find you and the girls so they can interview you, take your picture and put you on the radio for that great thing you and the girls are doing to save that poor little animal."

Sylvia nodded. She pointed at Emil, Arnold and Boris. "And what are these three eight balls doing while we're out in the hot sun getting donations?"

Steve pointed up toward the business district on Grand Street. "They'll hit all the businesses up and down Grand Street."

Sylvia shifted her gaze to Emil, Arnold and Boris. "I better see these cheeseheads out there hustling like me and the girls."

She kicked the cardboard box under the table with the stiff dried out dead cat in it. "What's in the box?"

Boris grinned. He reached into the box. He held the dead cat up right in front of Sylvia's face. "This is what will happen to the red fox if we don't save it."

Sylvia shrieked and jumped back. The other girls gasped when they saw Boris waving the dead cat around. Boris put Arthur back in the box then shoved it under the table and ducked out of Sylvia's reach.

"You moron. What're you doing with a dead cat?" she yelled.

Steve stood. "Calm down Sylvia. When somebody answers the door, you tell them you're trying to save the red fox and this is what will happen if the hunters get it. It'll work every time."

She bent over and looked in the box. "Aagh, maybe that's not such a bad idea Shorty."

She pointed at Boris. "Is this nitwit carrying the dead cat. I sure ain't and neither are any of the girls."

Steve shook his head. "No, I need Boris to carry the heavy boxes of bottles those guys collect from the businesses."

Sylvia gave Steve a suspicious look. "Who is carrying it?"

"Your little brother Mikey. He volunteered to help out. He said he likes animals."

She looked over at Mikey who was standing nearby. He nodded. He had a big grin on his face.

"Yeah, Sylvia. I get to carry Arthur and I get to help save the red fox."

Sylvia thought for a moment, then said. "Well, I guess that's Ok."

She glanced at Boris then at the dead cat. She shook her head, then said, "It takes all kinds." She went where the girls were holding their Save the Red Fox signs waiting for her. They marched away from the clubhouse waving the signs and chanting "Save the Red Fox, Save the Red Fox." with little Mikey carrying the dead cat hurrying to catch up.

Steve pointed up toward Grand Street. "You guys better get moving, hit those businesses, get back here to see all the fun."

Arnold looked puzzled. "What fun?"

"Yeah, what kind of fun is that walking around in the hot sun?" Boris said.

Steve grinned. "You'll see. Just get some pop bottles. We can turn them in for money."

The four boys watched the girls head out into the neighborhood. Arnold shook his head. "I don't know how you did it but you did it," he said.

"I had to see it to believe it," Emil added.

"I hope they don't hurt Arthur," Boris said.

"Gee, what a dummy," Emil said. "How can you hurt a dead cat?"

"Dead cats got feelings too," Boris said.

"How'd you pull it off Steve?" Arnold asked.

"I told you guys I had a plan. Just wait and see what happens. You guys better get going."

"And what are you doing while we're out in the hot sun?" Boris asked.

Steve sat at the table. He propped up a hand lettered sign Cash on a cigar box. "I'm staying here to direct operations and collect the money."

Emil, Arnold and Boris left heading up toward the Grand Street business district. Steve sat at the table in the shade with a smile on his face drinking a bottle of pop while he watched the girls visit the first house.

Sylvia went up on the porch with Mikey following carrying the box with the dead cat. She knocked on the door. A heavy set woman in a shapeless house dress opened the door. She looked at Sylvia and Mikey then at the girls waiting off the porch. "Whadda you kids want?"

Sylvia turned. She pointed to the signs the girls carried. "We want to save the red fox from getting shot by the hunters. Can you give us some pop bottles we can turn in to get money to save the red fox?"

The woman folded her heavy arms over her big breasts. She shook her head. She clucked several times. "Ain't that something? Somebody wanting to shoot a poor little fox. What's this world coming to?" She kept shaking her head and clucking. "Maybe I can give you some cookies for that poor little fella."

Sylvia shook her head. "No maam, we don't need no cookies for the red fox. We need some money so we can save it." She motioned Mikey to the door. "This is what will happen to the red fox if we don't save it. Show her Mikey."

Mikey yanked the dead cat out of the box. He held it up by the tail right in front of the woman's face. She let out a startled "Aagh." She slammed the screen door shut. She reached into the pocket of her house dress. She opened the door a crack. She held out a dime to Sylvia. "Here take this. Just get off my porch with that dead cat." She slammed the screen door shut. She locked it. She slammed the front door closed and locked it.

Sylvia held up the dime. "Just like picking cherries." She hurried off the porch. "Come on girls. Let's go get some more donations."

With Sylvia leading and Mikey carrying the dead cat hurrying to keep up, the girls marched from one street to another waving their signs chanting "Save the Red Fox, Save the Red Fox." They got money and pop bottles from women who wanted them to just get off their porches with that dead cat.

Emil, Arnold and Boris came back before lunch with donations and several baskets full of pop bottles.

"How'd it go?" Steve asked.

Arnold put coins into the cash box. "We got eighty two cents in money, and thirty seven pop bottles."

A few minutes later, the girls came in. Sylvia went to the table. She put coins into the cash box. She gave Steve a triumphant look. "Two dollars and twenty cents and seventeen pop bottles." She pointed to where Emil, Arnold and Boris were sitting in the shade. "How did those cabbage heads do or were they just sitting on their butts in the shade while we were out doing all the work?"

Steve pointed to the paper in front of him. "They did pretty good. Two dollars and eighty two cents and thirty seven pop bottles."

"Good thing," Sylvia said. "If they sat here all morning while we were doing all the work, there'd be some pretty good head busting going on about now."

She looked around. "Where are the radio and the newspaper guys?"

Steve gave her a pleasant look. "They'll be here after lunch. When you girls get back, you can work Marcy Street so that you stay close by and I can tell them where you are."

The girls and Sylvia went home for lunch. Emil, Arnold and Boris hurried home to eat while Steve sat at his headquarters post eating a brown bag lunch while looking over the sheets of paper on the table in front of him. Every so often, a grin spread over his face as he read and tapped the paper in front of him saying out loud, "The Master Plan." He leaned back in his chair with his hands clasped behind his head.

Emil, Arnold and Boris came back after eating.

"You guys better get going before the girls come back from lunch. Sylvia isn't in too good a mood. But stay around where you can see where the girls are going next. I'm sending them to Jimmy the Cheese's Mom's house first."

Boris was surprised. "His Mom hates cats."

"I know," Steve said smiling.

Arnold was puzzled. "Why you doing that?"

"Yeah, I don't get it," Emil said.

Steve tapped the paper on the table in front of him. "The Master Plan," he said. "You guys just stay close where you can see the fun."

"Ok," Arnold said. "Let's go you guys. The Genius wants to be alone."

The three boys went behind the clubhouse.

The girls came back from lunch. Sylvia went to the table to confront Steve. "Where are those newspaper and radio guys."

"They'll be here," Steve assured her. "They got a late start. They had some stuff to do before covering a big story like this."

Sylvia hesitated, then, said, "Ok, but they better show up Shorty."

"They will, but you and the girls better stay close so I can see where you are and send them over to watch you in action and, and interview you."

He pointed to a white house on the corner of the street two blocks from the clubhouse. "Go to that house first then go up that street so you will be close by where the newspaper and radio guys can find you."

Sylvia brightened at this. "Ok Shorty. Keep watching for those newspaper and radio guys so they know where we are."

"Will do," Steve said. "You can count on it."

Sylvia looked around. "Where are your meat head buddies? They better show up and help."

Steve pointed up toward the business district. "They got out early. They're hitting some more businesses."

Sylvia grunted then said, "I better see some action from those guys."

"You will, Sylvia, you will," Steve assured her, then thought, boy will you ever see some action Sylvia, real soon.

Sylvia formed up the girls. They marched off carrying their signs and chanting "Save the Red Fox, Save the Red Fox."

Little Mikey, Sylvia's brother, carrying Arthur, Boris's dried out stiff dead cat in a box, hurried to keep up with the girls as they headed toward the white house on the corner.

"Hey Steve," Arnold whispered from behind the clubhouse. "They gone? Is it Ok to come out now?"

"Not yet," Steve replied. "Sylvia may look and see you guys aren't out collecting bottles."

Sylvia and the girls go to the first house and went up onto the porch. Mikey followed. He stood behind his sister ready to hold up the stiff dried out dead cat to show what will happen to the red fox if they don't save it.

Sylvia knocked on the door. Jimmy the Cheese's Mother answered the knock. She was a small heavy set woman with black hair pulled back in a bun, old country style. She wore the same kind of shapeless dress that most ethnic women in the neighborhood wore. She looked at Sylvia then Mikey and the girls on the porch and on the walk carrying their signs. She had a puzzled look on her face.

"Hi, my name is Sylvia. We're all from the Mound Street Daisies . . ."

Before she could finish, Mrs. Roman said. "That's nice. Would you girls like some spaghetti? I just made a nice pot."

Sylvia shook her head. "Ah, no thank you. We are trying to save . . ." Mrs. Roman broke in saying, "I got some nice cookies I just made. Would you girls like some?"

"No thank you Maam. We are trying to save the red fox. Can you donate some . . . ?" That's as far as she got. Mrs. Roman opened the screen door. "Why sure I'll help that poor little fella. I'll make a nice lunch you can take to him."

"No thanks Maam. We're trying to save the red fox. We need to get some pop bottles so we can turn them in for money and, and buy a trap to save it from being killed by two bad men."

Mrs. Roman folded her arms over her ample stomach, shook her head and clucked as she listened to Sylvia.

"That poor little fella . . ."

Sylvia motioned for Mikey to come up to the door. "This is what will happen to the red fox if we don't save it."

Mikey reached into the box. He pulled the stiff dried out dead cat out and held it up by the tail right in front of Mrs. Roman's face. She screamed. She screamed again louder, then again, louder than before. Mikey panicked. He dropped the dead cat. It landed on the screaming, shrieking woman's feet. She looked down at the stiff dried out dead cat draped across her feet. She shrieked and screamed again and again, each shriek and scream louder than the one before. Later some people said they heard her screams and shrieks all the way down to Main Street, a half mile down Crow Avenue.

People came out of their houses to see what was happening. They ran toward Mrs. Roman's house. Sylvia's Mother heard the shrieking and screaming. She ran toward Mrs. Roman's house. Mikey began crying. He ran off the porch. Sylvia panicked. She jumped off the porch and ran toward the clubhouse. The girls screamed. They dropped their signs and ran in different directions.

Mikey ran toward his Mother. He pointed at the fast departing Sylvia. "She made me do it. Sylvia made me do it. She made me carry that dead cat to save the red fox."

Sylvia's Mother ran up on Mrs. Roman's porch. The screaming, shrieking woman pointed to the dead cat draped across her feet. She paused long enough to point down the street to where Sylvia was heading for the Daisies's clubhouse. "She did it, she did it," Mrs. Roman screamed again and again, "That big girl did it."

Sylvia's Mother grabbed one of the save the red fox signs. She was off the porch in one long jump. She hit the ground running following Sylvia toward the Daisies's clubhouse. Sylvia made it to the clubhouse. She was just opening the door when she saw her Mother running toward her waving the sign yelling, "I'll help you save the red fox."

Sylvia forgot about the clubhouse. She took off running toward home with her Mother hot after her waving the sign and yelling. She caught up with Sylvia. She began hitting her on the butt with the sign. "I'll help you save that red fox," she yelled with each whack.

"Ow," Sylvia yelled and did a hop and a skip then regained her full stride again. "I'll give you the Mound Street Daisies," Sylvia's Mother yelled again and again delivering one whack after another as she chased Sylvia into the house.

From where the four boys were sitting, they could still hear Sylvia's Mother yelling, Mikey crying and screaming and Sylvia yelling every time her Mother gave her another whack. "You ever go near that stupid clubhouse, you'll get worse than this." Then another whack and another yell from Sylvia.

Steve had a big grin on his face as he watched what was happening and listened as Sylvia's Mother ended her daughter's term as President of the Mound Street Daisies Club.

Emil, Arnold and Boris came out of the bushes where they had been watching. Steve had a big smile on his face. "Well, well, what do you know. We got our clubhouse back," he said.

Emil, Arnold and Boris were speechless as they listened to what was happening at Mrs. Roman's house and Sylvia's house.

"The Lord works in wondrous ways." Steve said. He shook the money box then went inside the clubhouse.

Emil, Arnold and Boris stood for a moment looking at each other. Then, Boris broke the silence by dancing around a couple times with his fists in the air and yelling, "Don't mess with the Mound Street Tigers," then followed Emil and Arnold into the clubhouse.

Steve was at the window. He pointed out. "Here he comes."

Chapter 30

Jimmy the Cheese's battered black Cadillac trailing blue smoke screeched to a stop behind a Police car in front of his Mother's house. Jimmy jumped out of the car. He ran into the house followed by Bosco and Usual. His Mother was laying on a couch. Several neighbor ladies were standing around clucking and shaking their heads while another woman was putting wet towels on the moaning Mrs. Roman's forehead.

"What happened? What happened?" he yelled at the ladies. A policeman was talking to the woman and taking notes. He started to say something to Jimmy. He was interrupted by one of the women who yelled at him, "Why ain't you out there chasing them crooks what did this?"

Jimmy yelled again, "What happened?"

When his Mother heard him, she began moaning louder than ever. "They tried to kill me Jimmy. They tried to kill your poor Mother." She gave off one long moan. The ladies watching clucked louder than ever and shook their heads harder than before.

One of the ladies outdid the others in clucking as she looked at Jimmy. "What's this world coming too?" she said.

"It's a real shame," said another woman.

"What, what?" Jimmy shouted. "What happened?"

The woman clucking the loudest gave Jimmy a sorrowful look. She followed with a sorrowful head shake, gave off a few more clucks and then said, "What's this world coming to when they throw dead cats at a poor old woman when she won't give them no money."

By now, Jimmy the Cheese was waving his arms and yelling louder than ever, "What? What happened?"

Another woman pointed to the moaning Mrs. Roman. "Who'd think it—a bunch of criminals throws a dead cat at her, tries to kill her just because she wouldn't give them money."

Jimmy took a handkerchief out of his pocket. He wiped his face. "My poor Ma. Who would throw a dead cat at a defenseless little lady trying to kill her just to get money?"

Jimmy looked down at his moaning Mother. "Who did it Ma? Who throwed that dead cat at you?"

Mrs. Roman looked up at her son. She moaned louder. "Oh Jimmy, it was awful. This little crook, musta been a midget, throws that dead cat at me after that big crook, a girl, kinda fat with big bushy hair, she musta been six feet tall, told that little crook to throw that dead cat at me when I didn't give her the money right away. It was a gang Jimmy, a gang of crooks."

The policeman grinned as he put his notebook away.

Jimmy's face contorted with rage. "Lousy dirty crooks," he yelled. "Picking on a poor defenseless woman. I'll get em. I'll get em."

He turned and yelled at the policeman, "Whadda you doing just standing here? Why ain't you out there catching that dangerous gang of dead cat throwing crooks?"

The policeman pulled Jimmy aside. "It was just a bunch of kids going around the neighborhood asking for donations of pop bottles they could take to the store, get some money to buy a trap and save a red fox out in the woods that some guys were gonna shoot."

Jimmy stared at the policeman. "Kids, kids, a red fox—they, wanna save a red fox? They wanna save it from some guys trying to shoot it?"

The cop nodded. "Yep, that's what some of the neighbors told me. The kids were walking around carrying signs, yelling something about saving the red fox from getting shot. They was asking people for donations to save it from being shot by a couple of bad guys."

Jimmy looked at Bosco and Usual who were avoiding his gaze.

The cop snapped his notebook shut. "Just a bunch of kids trying to do a good deed. That big girl was doing all the talking when someone answered the door. The little kid was carrying that dead cat around, was showing people what would happen to the red fox if they couldn't save it. When your Ma saw that dead cat, she screamed. The little kid panicked. He dropped the cat right on your Ma's feet. That started all the commotion. No harm done except to the stiff dried out dead cat that your Ma musta drop-kicked about twenty yards or so."

The policeman touched the visor of his cap with his fingertips. "Case closed Jimmy. See you later."

Jimmy was speechless for a moment as he watched the policeman leave the house. He looked at Bosco and Usual. "Saving the red fox huh?" He motioned with a nod of his head for the two men to follow him out the door. They left the house with the sounds of his Mother still on the couch moaning and groaning while the visiting ladies clucked and between clucks were saying:

"Such a thing."

"Awful."

"We could a been murdered in our beds."

Chapter 31

Jimmy the Cheese, Bosco and Usual were back in the poolroom below the Tavern. They sat at a table behind the counter. Bosco and Usual glanced at each other while Jimmy lighted a big cigar. He puffed hard on it sending clouds of smoke over the table. Both Bosco and Usual began coughing while trying to wave the cigar smoke away from their faces.

Jocko came in. He went behind the counter. He began coughing and waving the smoke away from his face. "Geez Jimmy, you trying to kill us all?" He sat at his desk still coughing and fanning the air.

Jimmy took a couple more puffs. "I'm thinking. I'm thinking about a lot of things. When you're the head of a mob, you got to do a lot thinking." He took the cigar out of his mouth. He jabbed it at Bosco then at Usual. "We have a couple problems here we got to take care of." He held up two fingers. He folded one finger in and now held up only one. "First, we got to get rid of that chicken stealing red fox before those kids can trap it, take it some place else before we can get it." Jimmy leaned back in his chair. He puffed toward the ceiling, then, slammed forward in his chair. He took the cigar out of his mouth. He pointed at Bosco then at Usual. "You guys know the mobster code. We can't let something like stealing my chickens go. We got to stop that fox. I got to get revenge. It's the code."

Bosco and Usual glanced at each other. Both shrugged.

"What we doin about it?" Bosco asked.

Jimmy banged the table with a closed fist. His eyes narrowed as he looked at the two men. He banged the table again. This time he kept the cigar in his mouth but pointed at the two men.

"I'll tell you what I'm doing. Somebody does me, I do em back harder. I'm putting out a contract on that chicken stealing red fox."

Bosco and Usual both had stunned looks on their faces.

Jocko had just taken a bite of a donut and a drink of his coffee. He spit both onto his desk when he heard what Jimmy just said. He stared at Jimmy in disbelief.

Jimmy turned to look at him. He glanced at Bosco and Usual.

"What's the matter with you guys? You never heard of a contract?"

He banged the table again, then again. "That's the code."

He leaned back in his chair puffing away on his cigar with a satisfied look on his face. He locked his two hands behind his head. "Whadda you guys think about that huh, huh?"

Jocko wiped up his spit out donut pieces and the coffee. He avoided looking at Jimmy.

Jimmy stood up. "Bosco, you and Usual go after that fox. We got to get it. That's the code when a contract is put out. You guys stay in that woods until you get that red fox before those goofy kids save it."

Bosco and Usual glanced at each other, shrugged and got up.

"Ok, Boss," Bosco said. "We'll get that red fox."

The two men left the poolroom. Bosco smacked Usual on the shoulder. "See what happens when you come up with some wild story like a red fox stealing Jimmy's chickens. Now, we're stuck slogging around in those woods trying to find some red fox before those crazy kids do."

Usual rubbed his shoulder. "How'd I know Jimmy would go bananas and, and put out a contract on a fox?"

Bosco smacked him again on the shoulder. "Now, we got to make like big game hunters just because we took a couple of Jimmy's chickens to make a few extra bucks and you tell Jimmy a fox took em."

Usual stopped. He rubbed his shoulder again. He looked at Bosco. "A couple of chickens? We musta stole twenty or thirty of them. What could I do. Jimmy finds out, he'll put a contract out on us. We'll be wearing cement overshoes. I had to blame it on the fox."

Bosco nodded. "I guess you're right but now he's gone berserk putting a contract out on a fox."

"Better the fox than us."

"Now we got to find a red fox and shoot it."

Bosco stopped walking. "You think Jimmy blew his top after that cat thing with his Ma?"

Usual shrugged as they went on walking. "I dunno but I never heard of anyone putting out a contract on a fox."

"I guess there's always a first time," Bosco said.

He stopped. He grabbed Usual by the arm. "I got an idea."

"What, what?"

"If those kids are trying to save the red fox and we're trying to shoot it, why not let the kids catch it. Let them do all the work, then, when they got it, we move in and bam, it's curtains for that fox."

Usual grinned. "Sometimes you surprise me Bosco. You use that head of yours for something besides a hat rack"

"Somebody got to do the thinking around here."

Usual thought for awhile as they walked. "It just may work. We keep an eye on them kids, watch where they set traps to catch the fox."

"Only this time, we don't get caught in them traps like we been doing," Bosco said.

Usual laughed. "That dummy Jimmy thinks Icepick Pete been setting those traps."

"Let's keep him thinking that until the kids catch the fox, then we move in, take it away from them," Bosco said.

"But, those kids are having as much trouble trying to catch that fox as we are. What if they do and it's not a red one like what we been telling Jimmy about a red fox stealing his chickens. What we do then?"

"Simple. We paint it red like I told you before. We show it to Jimmy. He won't know the difference. He's from Cleveland."

Usual thought for a short moment. "It just may work. At least, we won't have to be tromping in those woods all day long."

Chapter 32

Back at the poolroom, Jimmy the Cheese was at his desk writing in a tablet. He scribbled. He looked up, puffed on his cigar, then, scribbled again. This went on for several minutes. Jocko watched out of the corner of his eye while pretending to work. Finally, his curiosity got the better of him. He stuck his pencil behind one ear. He looked at Jimmy going through his routine of writing furiously, looking up, puffing huge clouds of cigar smoke, staring into space, then, putting more notes on the tablet.

"Whatcha doing?" He asked.

He tapped the tablet. "I'm working on a Master Plan." His voice dropped to a low pitch as he said Master Plan as though he was working on the plans for some secret military operation.

Jocko looked impressed. "A Master Plan. For what?"

Jimmy gave Jocko a long steady look. He tapped the tablet with his forefinger. "This is secret stuff. My Master Plan takes care of two of my problems." He held up one finger. "First, deals with the contract on that red fox what's been stealing my chickens." He held up another finger. "Second, I got a plan to trap Icepick, get him off my back once and for all."

Jocko looked impressed. "Can I see it?"

Jimmy shook his head. "Didn't I just say it was secret. You getting nosy or something?"

Jocko shook his head. "Ok, ok, so it's secret. If it's that secret, I don't wanna see it."

Jimmy grunted. "Good thing, you see it then I gotta shoot you."

Jocko's face paled. He jumped out of his chair. He backed away putting his hands out palms toward Jimmy in a defensive gesture. He closed his eyes. "I don't wanna see it. I don't even wanna see the cover. Don't show me nothin."

Jimmy the Cheese laughed. He pounded on his desk with both hands. He leaned back in his chair. He held his stomach as he laughed. He wiped tears from his eyes. He pointed at Jocko. "Gotcha, I gotcha good Jocko. That was a killer. Wait till I tell Bosco and Usual you turned white like that shirt you got on."

"That wasn't funny Jimmy," Jocko said. "I coulda had a heart attack you sayin that." Jocko sat at his desk. His hands shook as he went back to tallying betting slips. He kept glancing at Jimmy who was grinning at him.

"Man, that was some real funny stuff," Jimmy said.

"Yeah, yeah, Jimmy, real funny. It'd be hilarious I had a heart attack right here in your joint, the cops came in see all these betting slips scattered around underneath my body."

Jimmy looked serious. He nodded. "You're right Jocko. That happened, I'd have to drag your carcass out to my car, drive you to the donut shop—tell the cops you snuck out of work—pigged out on donuts, croaked right there."

Jimmy laughed louder than before. He slapped the desk with both hands. Tears flowed out of his eyes. He smacked his stomach. "Geez, that's funny stuff. I oughta go on the radio, telling jokes. I'd kill em. How about that—croaked in the donut shop."

Jocko jumped up. "I'm taking a break," he said and went out the door.

Still laughing, Jimmy yelled after him, "Hey Jocko, don't croak in the donut shop."

Jocko slammed the door. He jammed on his hat. He passed Bosco and Usual who were walking toward the poolroom. He gave them a quick glance as he went past without saying anything.

"Hey Jocko, how ya doin?" Usual said.

Jocko grunted. Usual turned to look at him as he stalked away.

"What's the matter with him?"

Bosco shrugged. "Who knows? Maybe Jimmy pulled his chain with one of his corny routines."

Usual nodded. "That'd make anybody mad."

They went down the stairs into the poolroom. Jimmy was wiping tears from his eyes.

"What's wrong with Jocko?" Usual asked.

"I laid one on him," Jimmy said laughing again. "He got nosy, asked me could he see what I was working on. I told him, I show you, I gotta shoot you."

"Maybe you shoulda showed him then shot him," Bosco growled.

Jimmy glanced at Bosco scowling as he shook his head.was.

"Awright, awright, what you guys got to report? What's happening with that contract on the red fox. You guys whack it yet?"

Both men plopped into chairs behind the counter. "Not yet Boss," Usual said.

"But we got a plan," Bosco said.

Jimmy threw his hands up. "Youse guys got a plan. I got a plan. Icepick got a plan. I'll bet that red fox even got a plan. Everybody got a plan. How about some action?" He jabbed a finger at Bosco and Usual. "That's all everybody does here is sit around making plans, no action." He lit another cigar. He puffed hard as he glowered at Bosco and Usual.

Bosco and Usual looked at each other. Bosco jerked a thumb toward Usual. "Tell Jimmy our plan."

Usual cleared his throat. "Me and Bosco got this plan."

"What is your plan?" Jimmy asked in a slow measured voice emphasizing each word.

Usual glanced again at Bosco. Bosco nodded a go ahead. "We got this plan. Instead of hunting that fox in the woods, we'll buy a trap and catch him."

Jimmy grunted. "I don't got enough trouble with a goof name of Icepick who's trying to steal my business, now I got two mobsters wanting to make like trappers."

Jimmy pounded on the desk. "I want action. I want to see some results. A contract is a contract. Get that fox. Burn down his house."

Bosco and Usual glanced at each other. "But, but," Bosco said. "Foxes don't got no houses."

"They live in a hole in the ground," Usual said.

Jimmy's face got red. His eyes bugged out. He stood. He banged the table with both fists. "I don't care if it lives in a tree. Find out where it lives and burn it down, or you guys can find another job. Maybe you'll be working for Pete upstairs in the booze joint. He might give you jobs washing dishes and mopping floors." He sat down hard in his chair. "Now get outta here and bring me a fox—a dead red fox. I got better things to worry about now like that crook Icepick."

Bosco and Usual hurried out of the poolroom.

"Now what we gonna do?" Bosco asked.

Usual shook his head. "I dunno, let me think."

The two men walked slowly up Crowe Avenue. They reached Marcy Street. Bosco stopped. He pointed to the house on the corner. "Ain't that where Jimmy's Ma lives?"

Usual stopped. "Yeah," he said. "That's where that kid dropped the dead cat on her feet."

Bosco had a surprised look on his face. "A dead cat?"

"Yeah, a stiff dried out dead cat."

"What happened to it?"

"I dunno. Somebody said Jimmy's Ma drop kicked it 20 to 30 feet into the bushes."

Bosco had a big grin on his face.

"What, what?" Usual asked.

Bosco was already heading for the bushes beside Mrs. Roman's house. He knelt down and parted the branches.

"Whatta ya doin?" Usual asked.

Bosco reached into the bushes. He pulled out the stiff dried out dead cat. "Here's our red fox."

Usual bent over and looked. "That's a dead cat. That ain't no fox."

"It is now."

"But, but it ain't even red."

"We'll paint it."

"You think we can fool Jimmy?"

Bosco grinned. "You kiddin me? Like I told you before, he's from Cleveland. I'll betcha nobody in Cleveland even knows what a red fox looks like."

Usual look around. "Nobody seen us so far. I'll get something from Mrs. Roman's trash to wrap it up in."

The two men hurried away from Mrs. Roman's house.

"How we painting it?" Usual asked.

"We'll buy some red paint at the hardware store."

Usual waited outside holding the wrapped up dead cat while Bosco went in the hardware store.

He went to the counter. A thin little man wearing steel framed glasses that perched on the end of his nose asked.

"Can I help you sir?"

"Yeah, I wanna buy some red paint and a paint brush."

"What kind of red paint? What kind of brush? There's different kinds of red paint—different kinds of brushes."

"I dunno, just some red paint and a brush."

The little clerk folded his arms across his chest. He looked Bosco up and down, then said, "Sir, the kind of red paint and brush you use depends on what you are going to paint red."

Bosco scratched his head. "I wanna paint a dead cat red."

The little clerk's jaw dropped open. He stared at Bosco. He pointed a finger at him. "Sir, did you say you want to paint a dead cat red?" I never heard of such a thing—painting a dead cat red."

Bosco leaned over the counter. He scowled at the little man. "Well you just did. You sellin me some red paint and a brush or not?"

The startled clerk backed away. "Yes sir, yes sir, red paint and a brush coming right up sir." He scurried to a shelf, grabbed a small can of red paint and a brush. He put them on the counter. He backed out of Bosco's reach. "That'll be plenty enough to paint a dead cat. Yes sir plenty enough. That's a dollar fifty."

Bosco glared at the uncomfortable little man as he put the money on the counter. The clerk managed a weak smile. "Thank you for your business sir," he said then hurried in to a back room. Bosco picked up the can of paint and the brush and left the store.

"What took you so long?" Usual asked.

"That little squirt clerk gave me a hard time about what kind of red paint, said he never heard of nobody painting a dead cat red."

Usual turned to look back at the hardware store where he saw the clerk and another man staring out the window watching them leave.

"You told him what we wanted the paint for?"

Chapter 33

Emil, Arnold and Steve were sitting in the clubhouse waiting for Boris. Emil sniffed the air. "What's that smell?"

Boris came in. His hair plastered to his head. "Hey, you guys, how do you like my new hairdo?"

"Yeah, but you're still fat," Emil said.

Boris jabbed a finger toward Emil. "Oh yeah. You ain't no prize package yourself."

Arnold got out of his chair and moved away from Boris. He pointed at him. "Boris is that you I smell?"

Steve wrinkled his nose. "Geez, Boris, you pour a whole bottle of hair tonic on your head?"

"You smell like Eddie Beracki," Emil said.

"I resemble that remark," Boris said as he went into his boxers stance. "Put up your dukes you little cabbage head. I'll murderize you. I'll punch you into next week." He danced around and threw punches into the air.

Steve banged on the table. "Will you guys cut it out? All of you sit down and shut up. I'll do the talking."

The three boys stared at Steve for a moment then sat down.

"Ok," Steve said. "I call this meeting to order right now. Let's go to the hardware store to see how much that trap costs. Maybe we can talk the owner in to give us a better price if we don't have enough money and we tell him what we want to do with the trap."

The four boys walked to the hardware store. They went over to the hunting and trapping supplies section where they looked at the different models of traps. Steve picked up one. "This one will trap the fox without hurting it."

The skinny clerk who waited on Bosco earlier came out of the back room with another employee. He waved his arms as he talked.

"Big guy, big tough mean looking guy buys this red paint and a brush. Says he wants to paint a dead cat red."

Arnold looked around. "Where's a clerk . . . ?"

Steve put a hand on Arnold's arm. "Shh, listen," he whispered motioning with his head toward the little clerk and the other man.

The four boys made like they were examining the trap while they edged closer to where the two men were talking.

"I never heard anyone painting a dead cat red," the other man said.

"That's what I told that big mean looking guy," the little clerk said. "I backed off when he looked like he was gonna rip my head off."

"Did he buy it?"

"Yeah, a brush too. He went outside and walked away with some little fat guy who was carrying something wrapped in a newspaper."

"What was wrapped up in the newspaper."

"I dunno know but something that looked like a tail dangled out."

"Musta been that cat those guys are gonna paint red," the other man said.

"Couple of real weirdos," the little clerk said.

The other man shook his head. "Takes all kinds. Maybe they belong to some kind of religious cult that paints dead cats red," the other man said.

The little clerk nodded. "Maybe," he said.

Steve put the trap back. "Let's go," he whispered to the other boys.

"Can I help you boys?" the little clerk called out.

"No thanks," Arnold said. "We're just looking."

Boris stopped outside the hardware store. He had a shocked look on his face. "Those two crooks got Arthur. They're gonna paint him red. They're turning him into a red fox. They'll probably shoot him—maybe torture him claiming he stole their chickens."

Arnold pulled Boris's arm. "Come on Boris. Arthur's already dead. They can't hurt him."

"Those two guys will take him to Jimmy the Cheese after they paint him red. They'll say he is the red fox that was stealing the chickens," Steve said.

"You think Jimmy the Cheese will shoot him?" Boris asked.

"Why would he shoot a dead cat?" Emil asked.

"Who knows what those crooks will do," Boris said.

"When they show Arthur to Jimmy the Cheese, they got no more use for him," Steve said.

"They'll just throw him away," Emil said.

Boris snuffled. He wiped his nose with his shirt sleeve. "Arthur saved my life. He helped get our clubhouse back. He deserves better than a trash can."

Steve patted Boris on the shoulder. "Don't worry. When they throw Arthur out, we'll go back after dark and get him out of the trash can."

Boris sniffled again. "I'd like to give him a proper burial, a heroes funeral for saving my life and helping us get our clubhouse back."

Emil and Arnold looked at Steve who shrugged and nodded. "Don't worry Boris, we'll get Arthur so you can give him a proper burial."

Boris wiped his eyes. "And, and, we'll give Arthur a heroes funeral too?"

The three boys glanced at each other and nodded.

"Yeah Boris," Emil said. "We'll do that too."

Chapter 34

Bosco and Usual drove out to the farm with Arthur the stiff dried out dead cat, the can of red paint and a brush on the floor in the back of the truck. They took Arthur into the shack where the new still bubbled and gurgled. He laid Arthur, the stiff dried out dead cat on a work table. He painted the cat a bright red then stepped back to admire his work. He made one more dab with the brush as though he had just painted a masterpiece. He tied a piece of rope to Arthur's tail then took the dead cat outside to a nearby tree where he tied the rope to a limb. The two men went inside the old farmhouse leaving Arthur swinging in the gentle breeze to dry.

The four boys were back in the clubhouse waiting until it got dark so they could rescue Arthur from the trash can behind Jimmy the Cheese's poolroom. Boris was pacing back and forth wringing his hands.

"Sit down Boris," Emil said.

"We'll get Arthur, don't worry," Arnold added.

Steve nodded. "When Jimmy the Cheese sees what he thinks is the red fox, Bosco and Usual will throw Arthur out."

Boris had a worried look on his face. "Maybe Jimmy the Cheese will go out to the farm to see what he thinks is the dead red fox. Then, then they'll throw Arthur away out in the woods. They do that, we'll never find him," he said his voice breaking.

Steve stood up. "Ok, ok. Let's go out to the farm. We'll find out what they're doing to Arthur. Maybe we can rescue him before they throw him away."

The boys rode out to the woods, hid their bicycles and crept through the underbrush to the old Miller farm. They stayed hidden in the bushes where they could see the farmhouse and the new shed where the whiskey making still was hard at work.

Steve pointed to a tree near the shed where Arthur was swinging in the breeze.

"It's Arthur," Boris said. "Those crooks ain't satisfied painting him red, they had to hang him upside down."

"They hung him up to dry," Emil said. "They ain't hanging him."

Boris started out of the bushes toward where the stiff dried out dead cat swung in the breeze.

Arnold grabbed his arm. "Where you going," he whispered.

Boris tried to pull away. "Leggo—I'm getting Arthur."

Emil grabbed Boris's other arm. "You crazy or something? You go there, those guys will shoot you dead just like Arthur."

"Yeah," Steve said. "After they shoot you, they'll hang you up there right with Arthur."

"And paint you red just like they did Arthur," Emil said.

Boris sat back in the bushes. "I changed my mind."

"Shh," Steve whispered. "There's Bosco and Usual." The two men came out of the farmhouse.

"How soon is Jimmy coming out to see the fox?" Usual asked.

"He's on his way," Bosco replied.

Usual laughed. "Bosco you sure are something else. Who else would a thought painting a dead cat red and passing it off as a dead red fox?"

Bosco grinned. "You gotta do what you gotta do. Let's see if it's dried enough."

They went to where Arthur, the stiff dried out now painted red dead cat was swinging in the breeze.

Usual touched it with his forefinger. "Lookin good Bosco."

Bosco poked the cat. "Almost done. Let's give it some more time."

The two men went back into the farmhouse.

"You guys hear that?" Arnold said. "Jimmy the Cheese is on his way."

Bosco and Usual came out of the farmhouse. Both men held pistols.

"They're gonna shoot Arthur," Boris wailed.

Emil clamped his hand over Boris's mouth. "Shut up. They'll shoot us they hear you."

The boys watched as the two men went to where the dead cat hung from the limb swinging in the gentle Summer breeze. Bosco poked Arthur. He looked at his finger. "He's dried up."

"Let's do it," Usual said. Both men stepped back from the stiff dried out dead cat. They raised their pistols. They each fired two shots into the swinging dead cat.

Boris tried to get up. Emil kept his hand over the struggling Boris's mouth while Steve and Arnold held him down. Boris grew limp. He slumped down.

He lowered his head. He wiped tears from his eyes. "They shot Arthur," he whispered in a voice choked with emotion.

Within a few minutes, Jimmy's battered Cadillac came into the farmyard and parked next to the old farmhouse. Bosco looked out the window. "He's here. Bring the camera."

The two men went out to where Arthur, now painted red, was swinging in the gentle breeze. Bosco stood beside the stiff dried out dead cat holding the pistol.

"Ok, take my picture. Then, I'll take yours."

Jimmy walked from his car to where Bosco and Usual were standing. He pulled up short when he saw Bosco standing in front of the hanging red dead cat. He stared at the dead cat then looked at Bosco.

"What we got here? The great jungle hunter?"

"We got him Boss," Bosco said as Usual took his place by the hanging stiff dried out dead cat. Bosco took his picture.

Bosco motioned for Jimmy to stand by the dead cat. "Ok Boss. You're next. I'll get your picture by the red fox."

Jimmy picked up both pistols off the table. "I'm a two gun guy," he said as he stood next to the hanging cat while Bosco took his picture. He stepped back a step. He raised both pistols and aimed at the cat. Bosco and Usual scurried away. Jimmy laughed and yelled "Bang, bang, bang. I gotcha you no good chicken stealing fox."

He put the guns on the table as Bosco and Usual came back to the dead cat.

"Ha, fooled you guys." He lit a big cigar, took a couple of deep puffs and blew the smoke out toward the dead cat.

"Nice going you guys. That takes care of one of my problems. Now we lay a trap for that crook Icepick, run him outta town. I'm heading back to the office. See you guys in a little bit."

Bosco and Usual watched as Jimmy got in his car and drove off leaving a cloud of blue smoke behind. Soon as he car was out of sight, Bosco raised a fist. "It worked."

Usual smacked Bosco on the shoulder. "We did it. We did it."

The two men shook hands because high fives haven't been invented yet.

Bosco took a pocketknife out of his pocket. He cut the dead cat down then went to the edge of the barnyard.

"It's bye, bye for you red fox. We don't need you no more." Bosco held the dead cat by the tail as he spun around like an Olympic hammer thrower. He let go of the dead cat. It sailed into the heavy underbrush.

Usual watched as the dead cat landed with a crash into the bushes. "We did it buddy. We fooled that big shot mobster," Usual said.

"Whoever heard of a contract on a red fox?" Bosco said.

"We did," Usual said. "Let's go back to town and celebrate."

The two men got into Bosco's old pickup truck and rattled out of the farmhouse driveway. The four boys waited until the truck was out of sight. Boris bolted out of their hiding place into the bushes where Bosco had thrown the stiff dried out dead cat. Emil, Arnold and Steve started into the bushes to help Boris find Arthur.

"Got him," Boris yelled holding up Arthur by the tail.

"What we going to do with him?" Steve asked.

"Let's bury him right here in the woods where he liked to roam around hiding from those two crooks," Boris said.

"Are you nuts or something Boris? He never roamed around here hiding from those guys. He wasn't a fox," Emil said.

"He's a cat. You found him stone cold dead in the woods," Arnold added.

"Well, he'd a roamed around in these woods if he'd a been a red fox," Boris said.

"Whatever—dead cat or dead fox. Let's bury him by the pond," Steve said.

Chapter 35

Jimmy the Cheese, Bosco and Usual were sitting in the poolroom. Jimmy waved a hand at the two men. "Good job you guys pulled whacking that red fox. I decided to go out of selling chickens so we can concentrate on the booze business and running that crook Icepick outta town." Jocko came hurrying into the poolroom carrying a bag of donuts. He poured a cup of coffee and sat at his desk. He offered the bag to the others. "You guys want donuts?' Bosco, Usual and Jimmy each reached into the bag and took a donut.

Bosco took a big bite out of his and said, "You must be getting soft Jocko springing for donuts." Jocko slurped his coffee and took a couple of bites out of his donut. He kept shaking his head while he chewed and drank. "You guys ain't gonna believe this," he said.

"Believe what?" Jimmy asked.

"It's weird, something you wouldn't a thunk of in a million years."

Jocko took a big bite out of his donut. He slurped more coffee. The three men waited with expectant looks on their faces. Jocko just kept shaking his head. "I'd a never believed it less I heard it with my own ears."

Bosco looked at Usual and Jimmy. He jerked a thumb toward Jocko. "This goof does it all the time."

Jimmy leaned toward Jocko. He pointed at him. "You telling us what you heard or do I have Bosco beat it out of you."

Jocko put his hands up. "Ok, ok, I'll tell you guys soon as I finish chewing up this donut. He took a long drink of coffee. He set the cup down, belched, wiped his mouth with the sleeve of his shirt. Bosco, Usual and Jimmy waited.

"A guy from the hardware store up on Grand Street was in the coffee shop. He was telling everybody in the shop to be careful. There's a bunch of religious nuts running around town. A couple of weird looking guys—long hair, beards, wild eyes came in the hardware store yesterday he says. They bought a couple of gallons of red paint and a bunch of brushes. Said they're painting all the animals in town red."

Bosco and Usual almost choked on the donuts they were eating.

Jimmy the Cheese shook his head. "What's this world coming to? Crazy people running around loose with cans of paint terrorizing poor animals. Next thing you know, they'll try to paint everybody red."

Chapter 36

Emil and Arnold were in the clubhouse when Steve came in. "You guys seen Boris this morning?"

The two boys shook their heads.

"He sure was down yesterday after we buried Arthur," Arnold said.

Emil shook his head. "How can a guy get so worked up over a cat that musta died a year ago and was painted red?"

Steve shrugged. "He was convinced Arthur saved his life when he tripped over him after the barn blew up."

"He'll get over it," Arnold said.

"Maybe we can find him another dead cat for a pet," Emil said.

Boris came into the clubhouse. He pointed at Emil. "Very funny, very funny Emil. The trouble with you is you got no feelings. You're a a cre-cre . . ."

"A cretin," Steve finished the word for him.

"Yeah, a cretin. You're a cretin."

"What's a cretin?" Emil asked.

"It's a dumb guy," Boris said real quick.

Arnold laughed. "What a couple of dummies you guys are don't know what a cretin is."

"Ok, smart guy, what is a cretin?" Emil asked.

"A cretin is a dumb guy from some country name of Crete," Arnold said.

Steve listened to the exchange. "Maybe you guys should read more. A cretin is a crude guy kind of like Bosco, Usual and Jimmy the Cheese."

"Speaking of those crooks, what happens when the red fox steals some more of Jimmy's chickens?" Arnold asked.

"Yeah, then Jimmy the Cheese will know the red fox is really not dead," Emil said.

"Bosco and Usual will go after the red fox again and we got the same problem trying to save it," Steve said.

Boris sat down. "We got nothing to worry about. My Dad said he was told that Jimmy the Cheese is out of the chicken business. The red fox got no more chickens to steal. Bosco and Usual won't have to hunt it no more."

"We won't have to worry about making money anymore to buy a trap," Arnold said.

"Yeah," Emil said. "Now we can spend our Summer having fun."

"We have to stay away from the pond," Steve cautioned. "It's on the property Jimmy the Cheese has."

"Bosco and Usual put up those no trespassing signs," Boris said.

Steve shook his head. "We saved the red fox but we sure haven't been able to do anything about that bunch of crooks."

"They came in the store again this morning," Boris said. "They made my Dad buy more of their rotten bootleg whiskey."

Emil banged his fist on the table. "We got to do something about those guys."

Arnold shook his head. "We're just some kids. What can we do when the cops won't do anything."

Emil held up a hand. "Wait a minute you guys. My Dad says the cops can't do anything because nobody will complain about Jimmy the Cheese and his gang."

Steve smacked the table. "If nobody will go to the cops, why don't we do it."

Boris had a startled look on his face. "Are you kidding or something?"

"Those guys are crooks," Arnold said.

"They got guns," Emil added.

Steve smacked the table again. "They may be crooks, they may have guns but we got right on our side."

"Big deal," Emil said. "We can be dead right we mess with those guys."

"I'm too young to die," Arnold said.

"Me too," Boris said.

Steve looked at the three boys. He pounded the table again. "What's the matter with you guys? We're the Mound Street Tigers. We fight injustice. We right wrongs wherever we find them. We can do some good for our neighborhood by going to the cops, tell them what those crooks are doing."

"I'd rather go swimming," Emil said.

"Me too," Arnold added.

Steve looked at Boris. "What about you Boris? Do you want to help get rid of those crooks, help your folks so they don't have to buy that bootleg whiskey and maybe go to jail if they get caught?" Boris was quiet for a long moment. He looked at the table. His shoulders sagged. He looked at Arnold and Emil then at Steve. He clenched his fists. He thrust his arms into the air. "I'm with you Steve. Let's go get those guys."

Steve shifted his gaze to Emil then Arnold. "What about you guys? You with us?"

Emil and Arnold exchanged looks. They both nodded.

"I'm with you but I don't like it," Arnold said.

"Me neither," Emil said.

"That does it," Steve said. He got up. "Let's go to the Police Station right now."

The four boys rode their bicycles into the downtown section. They parked outside the Police Station. They went inside. One Policeman sat at a counter reading a newspaper and drinking coffee. He was a big man with a red face. Bifocal glasses were perched at the end of his big nose. Another one, skinny, bald also wearing glasses was at a desk behind the counter tapping away at a typewriter.

Steve looked around. He walked up to the counter. The Policeman never looked up. Steve cleared his throat. Still no response from the Policeman.

"Excuse me Officer but . . ." Steve said. "The Policeman looked up before he finished the sentence.

The Policeman peered at Steve over top of his glasses. He glanced at each one of the boys.

"Whadda you kids want?" He raised an arm and pointed off to his right. "You looking for the Boy Scouts? They meet at the church on the corner." He came out with a big belly laugh. He turned to the skinny policeman at the desk. "You hear that Jasper. You hear that? I told em the Boy Scouts meet at the church on the corner. Ain't that funny?"

The skinny Policeman stopped typing. He gave the big Policeman behind the counter an irritated look. "Yeah, I heard it. I heard it and my name ain't Jasper. It is James."

"Ok, ok, Jimmy Jasper." "So it's James Jasper." He laughed again. He jerked a thumb toward the skinny policeman. "Ol James Jasper he don't got no sense of humor."

The skinny cop scowled and pounded harder on the typewriter.

Steve shook his head. "Sir, we're not looking for the Boy Scout meeting, we want to . . ."

The telephone rang. The big Policeman held up his hand for Steve to be quiet. He picked up the phone. "Police Station," he growled into the phone. His face brightened. "Oh yeah, Jimmy, Jimmy the Cheese."

He listened for a moment. "Ok, ok Jimmy. No more Jimmy the Cheese. How about James Mozzarella."

He laughed until tears flowed down his jowly face. He held the phone out. He turned to the skinny policeman. "Hey James Jasper." He pointed at the phone. "Jimmy don't like it I called him Jimmy the Cheese so I changed it to James Mozzarella. Ain't that some funny stuff or what" I should be on the radio telling funny stuff."

The skinny cop cringed. He just shook his head and went back to banging on the typewriter. The big cop went back to the telephone. "What, what Jimmy? You ain't mad are ya? You know I'm a big jokester."

Steve could hear shouting coming from the telephone.

"Ok, Jimmy Ok. Now don't get mad at a little joke."

The big cop listened for a minute. "Sure, sure Jimmy. We'll take ten tickets. Saturday nite right. We'll be there."

He hung up the phone. He clasped his hands in front of him. He peered at the four boys over the glasses perched on his nose.

Steve glanced at the other boys. "Ah sir, we were just curious what a police station looked like."

"So you guys wanna see what a police station looks like?"

"Yes sir."

The big cop got up. He turned to the other policeman. "Hey, Jasper, cover for me here. I'm showing these here boys what a police station looks like." He took a big key holder off a peg. "Ok, you guys follow me."

The four boys went after the big cop as he unlocked several doors leading back into the jail. "This here is where we keep the bad guys until they go to the State pen."

He pointed to one cell where a man with long hair and a tangled beard lay on a bunk. He motioned the boys close to the cell door. "That guy in there is Pistol Pete—one of the baddest guys around these parts. Likes to shoot people just for fun. I collared him myself. He put up a fight but I got him."

The big cop banged on the bars with the ring of keys. "Hey, Pistol Pete. Wake up. Come out, say hello to these kids."

He unlocked the cell door. The unkempt man stirred, sat up, stretched, looked over at the boys staring at him through the bars. He leaped off his bunk with a roar. He lunged through the cell door clawing at the air.

"I hate kids," he yelled. "Let me at em."

The startled boys turned and ran out of the cell block, through the station house and out into the street. As they went, they heard the big cop and the inmate he called Pistol Pete laughing. The big cop and the unkempt man appeared in the doorway of the station.

"Come back see us again kids," the big cop yelled after them.

"Yeah kids come back. I need some target practice," the man with the long hair and beard shouted.

Both men stood in the doorway laughing as the boys ran down the street. The four boys slowed to a walk after they turned a corner away from the Police Station.

"That was a great idea you had to go to the cops Steve," Emil said.

"We almost got killed right there in the Police Station with that nutty cop letting that crazy prisoner out," Arnold said.

"That was a set up," Steve said.

"Yeah, that cop thinks he's a real funny guy," Arnold said, "scaring us like that."

"I wasn't scared," Boris said. "That guy wasn't no Pistol Pete. That's Dirty Dewey. He comes in the store every so often, buys the cheapest wine we got."

"Why'd you run if you weren't scared?" Arnold asked.

"Who knows what a rummy with his scrambled brains will do," Boris answered.

"I didn't want to wait and find out," Emil said.

"Me neither," Arnold added.

Steve kicked a can off the sidewalk. "Now we know it's a waste of time to go to the cops if we have to talk with guys like that nutty Sergeant."

The boys walked on for awhile not saying anything.

"What we gonna do now?" Arnold asked.

Steve shrugged. "I dunno. I got to think about it."

"Why don't we just forget about trying to do something about those crooks," Emil said.

"Maybe Emil is right," Arnold said. "We tried but nothing seems to work out."

Boris stopped walking. "You guys can do what you want but I got to help my Ma and Pa. I don't want them to get in trouble having that rotten bootleg whiskey in the store.

"We been pouring it out when those guys deliver it. Your Ma and Pa won't get in trouble if it isn't in the store," Emil said.

"The more we pour out, the more those crooks think my Ma and Pa are selling. They'll just keep making them buy more and more until they go broke," Boris said.

Arnold shook his head. "Boy, this is a problem."

Steve stopped walking. He turned to face the other three boys. "Let's think about it until tomorrow. We'll meet at the clubhouse in the morning to figure out what we can do."

The next morning, Steve was the first one in the clubhouse. While he waited for the other three boys to come in, he made notes on a piece of paper, scratched out what he'd written, then wrote some more. Emil and Arnold came in and sat at the table.

Emil looked at the paper in front of Steve. "Whatcha writing?"

Steve put down his pencil. "I'm trying to come up with something that will help Boris's Ma and Pa and other business people who have to buy that bootleg whiskey from those crooks."

"Good Luck," Arnold said.

The door banged open. Boris rushed in. He waved some sheets of paper at the boys. "I got it. I got it," he said.

"What you got—athlete's foot?" Emil asked.

"Nah," Arnold said. "He's got a plan to kill Jimmy the Cheese."

"Why don't you guys stop trying to be funny. Listen to what Boris has to say," Steve said.

Boris bowed from the waist. "Thank you, thank you, Mr. President," he said and sat down. He spread the papers out on the table. He pointed at them. "This is how we get those guys and make some money too."

Arnold and Emil leaned over to see what Boris was pointing out.

"What. What?" Emil asked.

Arnold looked at Boris. "It's just a little newspaper."

"It's a newspaper put out by some guys at Goosetown—The Goosetown News," Boris said.

Emil sat back in his chair. "So what?"

Arnold folded his arms over his chest. "What's this dinky little newspaper got to do with us?"

Steve motioned for them to be quiet. He picked up the Goosetown News and looked through it.

"We can do the same thing," Boris said. "We can put out our own newspaper. We can write stories about those crooks. We can tell people all about what they're doing." He shook his fist. "We can show those crooks what the Mound Street Tigers can do when they get mad."

Steve leafed through the pages. He nodded. "Not a bad idea Boris—not bad at all."

Arnold scoffed. "We couldn't even raise enough money to buy a trap to save the red fox. How we getting enough money to start and run a newspaper?"

"Yeah, how?" Emil asked.

Boris pointed to ads in the Goosetown paper. "We sell ads to businesses just like these guys do right here. We can pay for the paper and make lots of money too."

Steve studied the ads. "Not a bad idea, not a bad idea at all."

Arnold and Emil still had skeptical looks on their faces.

"We can print the paper on my Dad and Mom's mimeograph machine. I know how to use it. I print our flyers for the specials we run every week."

"Who types up the stories and ads?" Arnold asked.

"My sister takes typing in school," Emil said. "We can pay her to do it after we take in some money. She'll be glad to get the practice."

"Then it's all set," Steve said.

Boris sat down. He folded his arms over his chest. "I'll be the editor because it's my idea."

Emil and Arnold shook their heads at the same time. "Steve got to be the editor," Arnold said. "He's read more books than any of us so he knows more about words."

"Boris, you can be a reporter cause you hear all the gossip people talk about in your Ma and Pa's store," Steve said. "Emil and Arnold will snoop around looking for stories too."

"We have to sell advertising first to get some money just like the big newspapers do, like the Akron News Press does," Boris said.

Steve wrote in the notebook on the table then said, "Good idea Boris."

He thought for a minute, then said, "We'll all go out, talk to businessmen then write stories about their businesses. People will read about them and will go buy their stuff. They'll make lots of money so they'll buy advertising in our great newspaper, The Mound Street News."

"What about those crooks?" Arnold asked.

"How we getting them with a little newspaper?" Emil asked.

Steve grinned. "You'll see. Our little newspaper will expose those crooks."

He stood. "Ok troops, we go out right after lunch. Each one of you visit as many businesses as you can. Get the word out about our newspaper. Find out about the businesses so we can write stories about them." He clawed the air. "Go get em Tigers. Get the stories."

The boys all let out a tiger roar.

Boris hurried home. He looked around in a closet until he found his Father's battered old briefcase. He dusted it off and put a notepad and a pencil in it. He searched around in the closet until he found his Father's old fedora hat. He put it on. He looked in the mirror. "Boris the Great, you look like a real businessmans." He gave the brim of the hat a final tug and left the house. He walked to the business district. He stopped when he saw a door leading to a second floor business. The sign on the door read, Millie's Fine Models.

My kind a business he thought. He opened the door, went up the stairs and rang a bell at the side of the door. A heavy set woman with frizzy dyed blond hair opened the door a crack. She peeked out at Boris.

"Yeah, whadda ya want?" she asked in a heavy too much whiskey too many cigarettes voice.

He tipped his fedora at the lady who was now eyeing him with suspicion.

"Hi. I'm Boris. I'm a reporter from the Mound Street News newspaper. I would like to write a story about your business."

The woman had a startled look on her face. "A reporter, a story about my business." She screeched.

Boris heard a growl behind the woman. A huge Doberman pushed past the woman. dlet out a ferocious bark. It pawed at the door trying to get out. Boris took one look at the dog. The woman unsnapped the door chain. "Sic em," she yelled.

Boris was already on his way down the steps taking them two at a time with the Doberman growling and nipping at his heels. Boris got to the door. He went out slamming it behind him. The Doberman was up on its hind legs pawing at the closed door growling and barking.

Boris ran down the middle of the street dodging cars and holding on to the fedora as drivers honked and yelled at him.

Chapter 37

Emil walked to a house where his Father told him a man named Stronoff sold all kinds of goods—toasters, irons, radios—out of his basement at real low prices. Two small trucks were behind the house. Two men were unloading one truck while another man was loading small boxes into the other truck. One of the men, older than the other one, short with a heavy moustache, wearing bib overalls and a straw hat, spotted Emil watching them working at the trucks.

"Whadda ya want kid?" he said in a gravelly voice. "You wanna buy something or you got something to sell?"

"Ah, no sir, I don't have anything to sell and I don't want to buy anything."

The man shifted the wad of tobacco from one cheek to the other. He let go with a steam of tobacco juice toward a scrawny cat that dodged just in time. He gave Emil a suspicious look as he went around to the cab of one of the pickup trucks. He took out a shotgun.

"If you ain't buyin or sellin something, whadda ya doin snoopin around here?"

Emil eyed the shotgun the man held. "I would like to talk to Mr. Stronoff."

"About what?"

"Ah sir, I'm from the Mound Street News newspaper. I would like to talk to Mr. Stronoff and write a story about his business. People will read about what a great business he has and come to buy lots of his stuff."

The man's eyes widened. "A spy," he yelled. The other man ran into the house slamming the door. The man raised the shotgun. "You're with that crook Icepick tryin to squeeze us outta our business. Jimmy the Cheese done told me about youse guys. You got five to get outta here and you done used up two."

Emil turned and ran. In two steps, he was up to full speed. The old man yelled "Boom, boom, and tell your Boss that lousy Icepick, I got a double load of buckshot waitin for him."

The old man laughed as he watched Emil disappear around the corner.

Arnold walked toward the cluster of shops at the corner of Grand and Crow Streets. He went past a house where several men came out singing and laughing.

"That guy Yossitch sure sells powerful stuff," one of them said.

Looks like Mr. Yossitch got a good business at that house Arnold thought.

He went to the back door and knocked. The door opened a crack. A man with a thin sharp featured face peered out. "Whadda ya want kid? You gotta be 21 to get in here so beat it." He slammed the door. Arnold knocked again. The door opened wider this time. "I thought I told you to beat it," the man snarled.

Arnold talked fast. "I'm from the Mound Street News newspaper. I would like to talk to Mr. Yossitch. I want to write a story and tell people about his fine business and the great beverages he sells here."

The door opened wider. A tall skinny man stood in the doorway. He turned and yelled back into the house. "Hey Charlie, quick, bring the shotgun. One of Icepick's crooks is out here just like Jimmy the Cheese said he'd come."

"You got it," a voice yelled back from inside the house.

Arnold quickly decided safety lay in another direction. Mr. Yossitz stood in the doorway holding a shotgun. He yelled after the fast moving Arnold, "Tell that no good crook Icepick he can't mess with honest businessmens."

Chapter 38

Steve decided to make his first sales call at the Southside tavern at the corner of Mound and Crowe Streets above Jimmy the Cheese's poolroom. He went inside and stood letting his eyes adjust to the dim interior. He wrinkled his nose at the smell of stale grease and beer. Several men were sitting at the bar. Jocko had just come in from Jimmy's poolroom to have lunch.

The bartender, a stoop shouldered thin man, bald except for white tufts of bristly hair jutting above and behind his ears, washed glasses behind the bar. He looked up when Steve came in. He shuffled to the end of the bar. He adjusted his glasses and peered at Steve. He pointed to the door.

"Hey kid—can't you read? That sign out on the door says you got to be twenty one to buy booze in here."

"Sir, I don't want to buy anything, I'm . . ."

The bartender cut him off. "You collecting money or something? Ok, here's a nickel now beat it."

"Sir, I'm not collecting money. I'm with the Mound Street News newspaper. I would like to help you get more business by writing a story about your fine place."

The old bartender leaned over the bar. He laughed and it came out more like a cackle. "We don't need no more business. I can hardly handle the goofballs we got coming in here now. Come back later, talk to the Boss."

The bartender motioned Steve closer. "Hey kid, you want a good story. Go downstairs to the poolroom. You can get a real good story about all the nuts that go in there, especially the chief nut they call Jimmy the Cheese. He owns the joint."

Jocko had taken a bite of his sandwich. He leaned closer to hear what the bartender was saying. The bartender turned to Jocko. "Right Jocko?" "That'd be a good story about them nut case characters that hang out down there, guys like Usual and Bosco."

Jocko looked startled. He took another bite of his sandwich, wrapped it in a napkin, got up, then said, "Right, right," as he headed for the stairs down into the poolroom.

The bartender pointed a crooked gnarled finger at Jocko as he went out the door. "He's another nutball what works for Jimmy the Cheesehead."

Chapter 39

Jocko hurried to the poolroom. He went to his desk. He picked up the telephone, then, looked around to make sure no one was nearby as he dialed. He waited, while the phone rang at the other end tapping the desk top with his fingers. Finally, someone picked up on the other end. Jocko looked around again.

A voice came on the line, "Yeah?"

Jocko pulled a handkerchief from his pocket. He wiped the sweat off his forehead.

"Hey, yeah?" the voice on the other end said again.

"Ok, ok, I'm here," Jocko yelled into the phone. "Lemme talk to Junie."

"I can hear ya Jocko, ya don't gotta yell."

Jocko drummed his fingers harder than ever on the desk top while he waited. He wiped his sweating forehead again.

The voice came back. "Hey, Junie ain't here."

"Where is he?' Jocko yelled into the phone. "We got a bad problem over here."

"You don't gotta yell inta the phone like I told you before. Hold on. I'll check."

There was another pause. Another voice came on. "Who wants to know where Junie is?"

Jocko lost it. He yelled into the phone again. "It's me Jocko. I gotta talk to Junie right away."

"Yeah, yeah Jocko. Why didn't you say so in the first place. This is Paulie. How ya doing over there? Junie ain't here."

Jocko got hold of himself. In an even controlled voice, he said, "Look Paulie, I gotta talk to him right away. It's real important."

"Everybody wants to talk to Junie," Paulie laughed. "So you wanna talk to Junie? Can you swim?"

Jocko heard laughing at the other end of the phone. "You guys hear that," Paulie said. "I asked ol Jocko who wants to talk to Junie if he can swim. Ain't that a rich one?"

"Paulie, you're a card, a real funny guy," Jocko heard another voice yell over the laughing.

Jocko bent over. He leaned his head on the desk. He held out the phone.

"Hey Jocko, Jocko. You still there?"

Jocko's hand shook as he put the phone to his ear again. He wiped the sweat off his forehead. He managed to gasp, "You mean, you mean Junie is . . . ?"

Paulie laughed again. "Gotcha huh Jocko. I gotcha a good one that time huh, huh?"

Jocko heard him say to the others on the other end, "I got ol Jocko again."

Jocko gave out with a long moan.

Paulie laughed. "Lighten up Jocko. It's not what you think. Junie's down in the Gulf fishing. He'll be gone all week Whadda ya want with him?"

Jocko never answered. His hand shook as he hung up the phone. Jimmy the Cheese, Bosco and Usual came into the office. Jimmy glanced at the pale sweating Jocko.

"What's the matter Jocko. You look like you stiffed a bettor and got caught."

Jimmy turned to Bosco and Usual. "You guys hear that? I told ol Jocko here he looks like he got caught stiffing a bettor. Boy oh boy, that's real funny stuff."

Bosco laughed. "Yeah Boss, you're one funny guy."

He elbowed Usual, "Ain't he?"

Usual nodded. "Yeah, yeah, sure. He's something else with that funny stuff."

Jocko wiped his sweating forehead. He pointed at Jimmy. "Nothing, nothing's wrong with me Jimmy cept that lousy crook Icepick had one of his goons, a little guy, a midget, wearing coke bottle glasses upstairs talking to that big mouth bartender old Joe. He was asking a lot of questions about your businesses.;"

Jimmy looked stunned. "You mean he sent one of his gang right here to the joint upstairs to pump people about my businesses?"

He pounded the counter with his fist. "That's it. That's it. This means war. He came around the counter to his desk. He grabbed the phone. "I'm calling Uncle Junie right now. He's got to get that idiot nephew of his Icepick Pete out of here."

Jocko shook his head. "No use calling Uncle Junie. He ain't there. He's down in the Gulf fishing for the next week. You wasn't here so I called to tell him what happened."

Jimmy sat at his desk. He leaned his head onto both hands, "I gotta think, I gotta think," he kept saying over and over. He looked at Usual and Bosco. He jabbed a finger toward the two men. Ok, ok. The gloves are off. No more nice guy. You guys find that pipsqueak Icepick Pete. Bring him in. We'll send him back to Uncle Junie. Don't hurt him. Rough him up a bit but, no bruises what show. You know what I mean?"

Chapter 40

The four boys met back at the Mound Street Tigers clubhouse.

"How'd you guys do?" Steve asked.

Each boy told of his encounter with the business owners.

Steve tapped the table with his pencil. "Interesting."

"What we doing now?" Boris asked.

Steve banged his pencil onto the table.

"We go ahead with the newspaper. We write the stories anyway. When people read the stories, other businessmen will want to advertise in our paper because we exposed some shady businesses."

For the next two days, the boys were busy writing their stories. Steve edited each one as the boys completed them. They finally finished putting the paper together. Emil's sister typed everything and Boris mimeographed the first edition of the Mound Street News on the table.

Steve stood. He picked up a paper from the pile. He looked at it and grinned. "Boy o boy. This should do it. Let's all take a bunch and hand them out in the neighborhood. I'll take the business district up at Grand and Crowe. You guys go back to where you got the stories. Leave the papers. We'll go back tomorrow after people read the stories about Jimmy the Cheese's businesses and how he makes honest people like Boris's Mom and Dad buy his rotten bootleg whiskey. They'll like the paper so much, they'll buy ads in it and we'll make a lot of money."

Chapter 41

Boris picked up his briefcase, put copies of the paper in it, cocked the battered fedora at a jaunty angle, then went back to the restaurant below Millie's Fine Models. The same tall thin man with a prominent nose and big Adams apple sat behind the counter at the cash register reading a newspaper. Boris cleared his throat. The man never looked up. Boris cleared his throat again. "Ah sir."

The man glanced up from his newspaper. He looked Boris up and down. He nodded. "Ain't you the kid that was here the other day, Millie sic'd her dog on?"

Boris nodded. "Yessir, but I was too fast for him."

"Good thing. That Millie's Doberman sure likes to sink his teeth into fat guy's butts."

The man laughed. "I can just see you running down the street yelling your head off with the Doberman clamped on your butt."

The man slapped the counter. He laughed again. "Boy, that's a real kneeslapper."

Boris shifted from one foot to the other as he rubbed his butt and glanced out the front window.

"Don't worry kid. Millie's not up there and she's got Buster locked up. Whadda you want anyway?"

Boris kept glancing toward the front window.

"Ah sir, I would like to leave some copies of our newspaper, the Mound Street News, here on your counter for your customers."

The man shrugged his shoulders. "Sure, leave em."

Boris left a stack of papers on the counter. He hurried out of the restaurant looking toward the door leading upstairs to Millie's Escort Service.

The man in the restaurant picked up one of the papers. He read the headline of the story about Millie's business. He whistled.

"I got to show this to Millie," he said out loud, the added. "Maybe that guy's with some secret Guvmint agency." He shook his head. "Nah, the guy's too dumb looking to be a Fed."

Chapter 42

Emil and Arnold went back to the neighborhoods where Stronoff and Yossitch had their businesses. They left copies of the Mound Street News on the porches of houses and handed them out to other businesses in the neighborhood.

Steve took an arm full of the papers and passed them out at businesses around the corner of Mound and Crowe Streets. A police car was parked near the corner with the officer inside drinking coffee and eating donuts. He watched Steve leaving papers at businesses on both sides of the street. When Steve was coming up on the police car, the officer waved him over.

"Whatcha passing out there Kid?" He laughed. "Nothing illegal I hope."

Steve went to the driver's side. "No sir, it's nothing illegal. This is the first edition of our new neighborhood newspaper, The Mound Street News."

He handed a copy toward the officer. "Would you like a copy sir? The first edition is free."

The officer took the paper. "Sure, why not if its free."

He watched Steve continue down the street leaving papers as he went. "Kids a hustler," the officer said out loud. "Gotta hand it to him."

He leaned back in his seat, tipped his cap back, took a bite out of a donut, slurped some more coffee and began reading the Mound Street News. After reading the first page, he sat upright. "My of my," he said out loud. "This is some dynamite stuff."

He finished reading the Mound Street News. He ate the last piece of his donut then drained the coffee cup. He leaned back in his seat. "Wow, who'd a thunk it right here in this neighborhood."

The officer pulled his cap down, checked its position in the mirror. He folded the paper and put it on the seat next to him. "This I got to show Sgt. O'Malley."

He slipped the car into gear and made a tire screeching u-turn in front of oncoming traffic. He waved at the braking, swerving, yelling drivers shaking their fists at him.

"Urgent Police business," he yelled back at them.

Chapter 43

The next morning the four boys met at their clubhouse.

"Ok you guys. We did it," Steve said. "Now, let's go back to the same neighborhoods, talk to the businessmen, see if we can get some ads for the paper. Leave a paper at each of Jimmy the Cheese's businesses. That way we make sure they see the stories. But, be careful."

"Yeah, those guys won't be too happy with the stories we wrote about them," Arnold said.

"And they got shotguns," Emil added.

"And Dobermans," Arnold said.

Boris got up. "Ha, nobody, not even those crooks with their shotguns and mad dogs, can scare Boris the Great. I'm going right back to Millie's Fine Models and personally give her a copy of our paper. If that Doberman even looks at me, I'll give it the famous Boris the Great one two punch right in the schnozzola."

Boris danced around the clubhouse throwing punches into the air.

"Take that and that and that," he yelled as he punched and kicked the air. "I'll murderize it with my karate kick."

A dog growled outside the clubhouse. Boris froze with one arm in midair and one leg out in a karate kick.

"What's that?"

Emil laughed. "Maybe Millie sent her Doberman here after you."

The growling stopped.

"That ain't funny, Emil," Boris said. "I could a been killed by that mad dog."

"You weren't that time but you go near her place again, you may be," Arnold said.

Steve stood. "Ok you guys Let's get going. We got business to do today."

Emil, Arnold and Steve left the clubhouse. Boris hung back. He poked his head out the door. He looked around.

Emil laughed. "You can come out now Boris the Great. Millie's Doberman ain't here."

"You're a real funny guy Emil," Boris said as he looked around then followed the three boys.

Emil went to Mr. Stronoff's house first. He figured he would leave the Mound Street News on the porch where it would be found right away. He saw the two Police cars and a big truck parked at the side door. Two Policemen came out carrying boxes of merchandise. They put the boxes in the truck. One of the Policemen took off his hat and wiped his sweaty brow with a handerchief.

"Man oh man," he said. "That Stronoff had a regular department store in there."

Just then, two more Policemen came out holding a struggling, shouting Mr. Stronoff.

"I'm innocent," he yelled. "I saved a lot of box tops. That's how I got all this stuff."

"Yeah, yeah sure," said one of the cops holding him. "And I'm the King of England."

The two Policemen managed to get the still yelling Mr. Stronoff into the Police car. Once inside he quieted down.

The Policeman in the right front seat pushed his cap to the back of his head.

"For a skinny old guy, that Stronoff is a strong one."

The Police car drove slowly down the long driveway toward the street. When it passed Emil, Stronoff began yelling out the open window and shaking his fist at Emil.

"I know you, you lousy crook, writing those lies about me, working for that creep Icepick Pete so he could steal my honest business. I'll get you for this."

The Police car drove out and turned onto the street with Stronoff still leaning out the window shaking his fist and yelling at Emil.

The Policeman driving shook his head." Wonder what set him off again?"

The other Policeman shrugged. "I dunno. Maybe he was yelling at that kid we just passed."

Chapter 44

When Arnold got close to Mr. Yossitch's place, he saw some vehicles in the driveway parked near the back door.

"Mr. Yossitch is sure doing a lot of business today," he thought as he walked down the long driveway toward the house where he planned to leave the Mound Street Newspaper on the front porch.

"Oh, oh," he thought when he saw the two Police cars and a truck parked at the back door. Two Policemen came out of the house each carrying two jugs they put in the back of the truck.

"Almost full," one of the Policemen said.

Two other Policemen were dragging a struggling, shouting and swearing Mr. Yossitch out of the house.

"Hey, give us a hand with this guy," one of the Policemen yelled to the other two officers. The four officers finally were able to get Mr. Yossitch in the back of the Police car.

"Geez," one of the Policemen said. "You wonder what makes an old guy like him so strong."

One of the other officers shrugged. "Maybe he drinks a lot of his own stuff. I heard it's pretty good."

Arnold started to step back in the bushes as the Police car drove by but Yossitch spotted him before he made it. Yossitch leaned out the window. He shook his fist and yelled at Arnold.

"You, you low down snake in the grass working for that no good crook Icepick Pete. Jimmy told me all about you guys. I'll get you for this."

Arnold watched the Police car turn onto the street and disappear toward the Police Station. He hurried back to the clubhouse thinking, I got to tell the guys about this. We're in big trouble now. Those crooks will be out to get us.

Chapter 45

Boris hurried toward Millie's Fine Models. He went over in his mind what he would do if she sic'd the Doberman on him again. I'll give it a karate kick. That'll slow it down. Then, I deliver my special Boris the Great killer punch right to its chops. He executed a fancy step, a couple of karate kicks and hit the air with several rights and lefts.

He passed a couple of grizzled old winos who stared as he went by. One of the winos nudged the other one. He pointed to Boris kicking the air and delivering punches as he executed a series of fancy footwork steps.

"I thought we got the shakes real good from drinking that cheap Jimmy the Cheese's stuff," the man said. "Look at the guy. He makes us look sober."

Boris reached the building where Millie's Model business was located. The outer door to the stairs was open.

A mailman tapped Boris on the shoulder. Boris let out a yell and jumped sideways away from him.

"Oops, sorry I scared you buddy but there's no sense going up there anymore." he winked at Boris. "If you know what I mean for."

The mailman saw the bewildered look on Boris's face. He looked at the Mound Street News copies Boris was clutching. "Sorry, I didn't know you was just a kid delivering papers."

Boris watched the mailman hurry down the street then looked in the doorway and up the steps. Papers were scattered on the stairs. The door to Millie's business was wide open. He thought for a moment, remembered the Doberman then decided against going up the stairs. He went into the restaurant. The same thin man with the big Adams apple was sitting behind the counter reading a newspaper. Boris cleared his throat a couple of times but the man never looked up from his paper.

Boris shifted from one leg to the other as he kept glancing out the restaurant window toward the stairs to Millie's business.

"Ah sir," he finally said.

The man looked up. "Yeah, whadda ya wanna order?"

Boris pointed toward the stairway leading to Millie's business. "Ah sir," he said.

The counterman peered up at him. "Oh yeah, I know who you are now. You was the guy what left those goofy newspapers the, the . . ." he snapped his fingers, "the Mud Street News or something like that."

"Mound Street News, Sir, the Mound Street News."

"That's what I said, the Mud Street News."

The man laughed. He reached under the counter and pulled out several copies. "Here's what's left what you gave me the other day. I gave Ol Millie a copy. She read it, grabbed a couple more and went berserk, nuts, completely bananas. She ran back upstairs. I hear her throwing stuff around then she came racing down here carrying a couple of suitcases with the big Doberman right after her growling like he's gonna hunt someone down."

Boris stared at the man. He opened his mouth but nothing came out.

The man pointed at the back of the restaurant.

"She came in here, ran right through the restaurant out the back door screaming and yelling, she ever sees that crook newspaper guy again she'll use her thirty eight, make him look like a piece of Swiss cheese."

The counterman grinned. "I'll tell ya something buddy. If I was you, I'd make myself real scarce for awhile, her waving that thirty eight around and her with that Doberman to boot."

Boris stared at the counterman. He tried to say something but nothing came out. He stepped back, then, turned and hurried out the door.

The counterman laughed. He yelled after Boris, "Hey buddy, you wanna tell me where Millie can get hold of you?"

One step out the front door of the restaurant, Boris was already running. He held the old fedora on his head as he ran yelling, "She's gonna murderize me."

Chapter 46

Steve walked to the business district at the corner of Grand Street and Crowe Avenue. He went into the Southside Tavern. He stood for awhile just inside the door letting his eyes get used to the dark musty interior. The place smelled the same as it did the other day—stale beer and grease, and frying hamburgers and onions. Joe, the old bartender was at the far end of the bar washing glasses. The place was empty except for four men sitting at the bar staring into their glasses of beer. A real happy place Steve thought. The bartender looked up. He wiped his hands. He waved at Steve then shuffled to the end of the bar to where Steve waited.

He pointed a crooked finger. "I read your paper," he laughed. "Youse guys opened a can of worms with that newspaper of yours. Lots a people I talked to read it too and I might say with more than just a little interest. Yes sir, I might say that."

Steve smiled. "Thank you sir."

The bartender looked over his shoulder. He lowered his voice. He grinned. "You wanna talk to Sam the owner of this joint? He may just wanna advertise with youse guys."

Steve nodded. "Gee, thanks. That's great. Is he here now?"

Joe, the bartender chuckled. "He sure is here. I mean he's downstairs." He pointed toward the poolroom below.

"Thank you sir. Thank you," Steve said as he turned and hurried out the front door.

The bartender watched Steve go. "Yeah, he's here all right," he said out loud as he shuffled back to the far end of the bar chuckling as he went.

Steve went around to the back of the building. A bald headed heavy set man with a bushy moustache and an unlit cigar in his mouth was sweeping up paper and debris at the top of the steps leading down to the poolroom. He was not in a good mood as he muttered and swept and picked up clumps of paper and stuffed them into a trash bag grunting as he bent over and straightened up.

Steve watched for awhile. He cleared his throat. "Ah Mr. Sam," he started. The man looked up.

"Whadda ya want kid? I'm busy right now," he growled. He kicked a waste basket. It sailed into the street. He was muttering loud enough for Steve to hear. "Bunch of crooks that Jimmy the Crook Cheese and his no good gang?"

Steve hesitated for a moment, then decided to press on. He took a pencil from behind his ear. He opened his notebook. "I'm from the Mound Street News newspaper . . ."

Mr. Sam leaned on the broom handle. He nodded as he looked at Steve. He chewed on the cigar stub as he shifted it from one side of his mouth to the other. He nodded.

"Yeah, yeah, I know who you are. You're the guy from that kid's newspaper that brought the cops down on Jimmy and his gang. Now I don't got nobody renting this joint."

"What happened to Mr. Cheese?" Steve asked.

Mr. Sam snorted. The cigar stub almost popped out of his mouth but he caught it just in time.

"Hah, Mr. Cheese hah. Mr. Stiff you mean, got me for two months rent. Yeah, Mr. Stiff is a better name for that guy." He waved his hand around at the debris. "Look at the mess I got." He pointed down the steps toward the poolroom. "You should see what the cops did down there."

"What happened to Mr. Cheese er Mr. Stiff?" Steve asked again.

"Got away. Somebody musta tipped him off. Him and them two stumblebums, Bosco and Usual, beat it back to Cleveland. The cops got that other guy, the tall skinny one, Jocko. He was trying to eat some betting slips in between bites on a donut and slurping coffee to wash em down. The cops got him over to City Hospital. They pumped his stomach for evidence. Chief said all they got was a lot of chewed up donuts and paper."

The man shook his head as he went back to sweeping. "Yeah, that Jimmy the Stiff musta gone bananas. Old Joe, my bartender said the Stiff and those two meatballs working for him ran through the bar when the cops came yelling something about Icepick, Icepick Pete."

He looked at Steve. "You know kid, the whole world is full of nuts and weirdos and I had to rent my place to one of em." He kept shaking his head as he went back to sweeping and picking up the mess in the back of his building.

Chapter 47

Steve hurried back to the clubhouse where Arnold and Emil waited. They had glum looks on their faces. Steve sat down. "Boy, our newspaper sure did it."

"Yeah, more like it did us," Arnold said. "Old man Yossitch got busted after our story about him was in our paper. He saw me when the cops were taking him away. He yelled that he would get me. Claimed I worked for a crook named Icepick Pete to run him out of business."

Emil shook his head. "I don't know about this newspaper business. When I got near Stronoff's place, the cops were there taking stuff out, loading up a truck. It took two of em to drag that old guy out of his house and four of them to get him into the Police car. He was fighting and yelling all the way into the Police car about that crook Icepick Pete writing bad stories about him. I tried to hide in the bushes when the Police car left but Stronoff saw me. He went crazy, leaning out the window swearing and shaking his fist yelling that he's gonna get me."

Boris rushed into the clubhouse. He threw his fedora and battered old briefcase into a corner. He dropped to his knees and crawled under the table.

Steve looked under the table. "What's the matter Boris? What happened?"

Boris let out a long sigh. "You and your newspaper. She's gonna kill me, that's what, make me look like a piece of Swiss cheese with her thirty eight after that Doberman chews me up." He let out another long wail. "She'll murderize me. I'm goin to Guatemala."

He crawled out from under the table all the way to the door then got up and ran out of the clubhouse yelling, "I'm a gonner. I'm gonna be dog food."

Emil leaped to his feet. He ran out the door yelling. "I'm heading for Mexico."

Arnold was right behind him yelling, "Me too," as he ran out of the clubhouse.

Chapter 48

The next morning, Steve was in the clubhouse real early. He had a newspaper spread out on the table. He had a big smile on his face when Arnold poked his head in the door and looked around.

"Anybody looking for me?"

Steve shook his head. "Nobody yet."

Arnold came in and plopped into a chair.

Steve laughed. "I thought you was heading for Mexico with Emil."

"It ain't funny Steve. We are soon as we can get some money."

"Where's Boris? Is he on his way to Guatemala?"

Arnold shook his head. "Naw, not yet. He doesn't know where Guatemala is. He's coming in to ask you where it is."

"Where are they now?"

Arnold pointed toward the corner. "They're hiding in the old tool shed behind the store."

Steve tapped a finger on the newspaper open in front of him. He had a big grin on his face.

"Tell them to come in here. I've got some good news."

Arnold was half out of his chair. "What kind of good news? You know where Guatemala is? You can loan us money to get out of town?"

Steve shook his head. "It's better than that. I'll tell you when you're all here."

Arnold rushed out of the clubhouse. Within a few minutes he was back with Emil and Boris.

The three boys crowded around the table.

"You got a ticket to Guatemala for me?" Boris asked.

Emil held out his hand, "Two tickets to Mexico?"

Steve, smiling broader than ever, shook his head. "No, no and no again." He turned the spread out newspaper around so the boys could read it. He tapped the headline. "Read it you guys. We're off the hook."

174

Arnold leaned over. He read the headline. "Officer O'Malley Smashes Gang."

Emil pointed to the picture on the front page showing a beaming Sgt. O'Malley standing with several politicians shaking hands with the Mayor.

Emil read the caption under the picture. "Sgt. O'Malley is congratulated by the Mayor for risking his life to singlehandedly break up the notorious Jimmy the Cheese gang."

Arnold pointed to the story under the picture. He read, "According to the modest hero Sgt. O'Malley, Jimmy Roman, alias Jimmy the Cheese, and his gang had their escape route planned. I chased them out of town. We had a fierce gun battle but their souped up cars pulled out of range."

Boris read further. "The Mayor said we owe this fine brave officer, Sgt. O'Malley, a debt of gratitude for risking his life for ridding our fair city of these desperate criminals."

Emil pointed to another picture on the front page showing Sgt. O'Malley smiling as he held a handcuffed snarling skinny little man by the back of his shirt collar.

Emil read from the story underneath the picture. "While the notorious gang leader, Jimmy the Cheese got away, Sgt. O'Malley, singlehandedly, at great risk to his life, captured a vicious and dangerous criminal known as Icepick Pete who was robbing paperboys in his bid to takeover the mob activity in our city. Sgt. O'Malley described how Icepick Pete pulled a Tommy gun on him but was able to get only one burst off before the courageous officer disarmed him and wrestled him to the ground."

The four boys looked at each then broke out laughing.

"Well," Steve said. "We can all sleep well tonight with the courageous Sgt. O'Malley guarding our town."

"Yeah," Boris said. "Let's go swimming."